EXTRA RAUNCHY
CHILDREN OF THE CATACOMBS

T. STYLES

NATIONAL BEST SELLING AUTHOR OF *RAUNCHY*

Library of Congress Control Number: 2013951664
ISBN 10: 0989084507

ISBN 13: 978-0989084505

Cover Design: Davida Baldwin www.oddballdsgn.com
Graphics: Davida Baldwin
www.thecartelpublications.com
First Edition

Printed in the United States of America

ARE YOU ON
OUR EMAIL
LIST?

CHECK OUT OTHER TITLES BY
THE CARTEL PUBLICATIONS

What's Up Fam,

I know ya'll anxious to get at this one, and I'ma make it quick but words need to be said about this joint. "Mad Maxxx: Children of the Catacombs", in my opinion is, "Out The Box Original". Twisted T. Styles takes you on a journey through the underworld. As I read this novel, my head began flooding with visions of this dark and mysterious place. And to make it more official and original, T. Styles sketched up her vision of The Catacombs so that her readers would know exactly where she was going. We included it in the beginning of the story so make sure you check it out!

Keeping in line with tradition, we want to give respect to a vet or trailblazer paving the way. With that said we would like to recognize and pay respect to our fellow author and legend:

Tom Clancy

Tom Clancy is a world renowned author who has penned classic novels such as: "Without Remorse"; "Rainbow Six"; "The Hunt for Red October" and his upcoming novel, "Command Authority", being released posthumously on December 03, 2013. Thank you for sharing your gift with the world Mr. Clancy. R.I.P.

Ok, go 'head and dive in! I'll get at you in the next novel.

Be Easy!
Charisse "C. Wash" Washington
Vice President
The Cartel Publications
www.thecartelpublications.com
www.twitter.com/cartelbooks
www.facebook.com/cartelpublications

I believe in a world full of animated people. And I'm not talking about vampires, goblins and ghouls. But they are characters, just as mysterious and enchanting.
Take my hand. I want to show you.

- T. Styles

THE CATACOMBS SKETCH BY T. STYLES

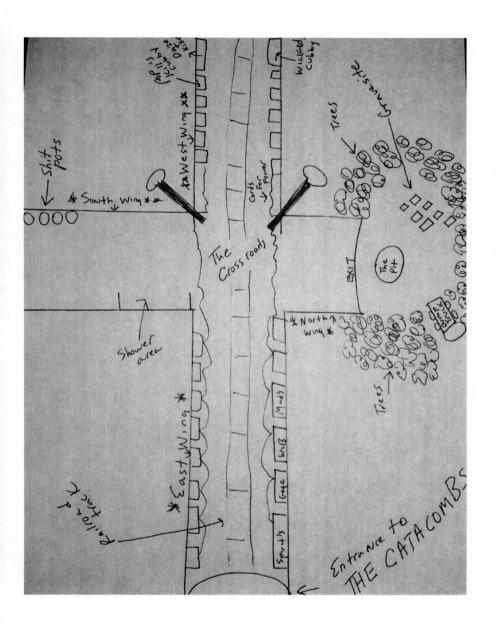

PROLOGUE

Present Day

Madjesty's chest felt as if it were about to explode, as she swam quickly to the top of the murky water. Her eyes burned as the filthy liquid covered her face, and her body felt heavy. Madjesty would've allowed the water to enter her lungs, despite possibly drowning, if there was the slightest chance that calling *her* name would reunite them. That calling her name would ensure that her love was still alive.

When she saw the moonlight radiate against the surface of the water above her head, a sense of relief took over because she was almost there. But would Everest be waiting? Or would God take her too, like he did every other person she loved?

The moment Madjesty's face broke the river's barrier; water crawled down her nose and throat, threatening to choke her by filling her lungs. She coughed a few times, clearing her passageway before she was finally able to yell, "Everest"— she hacked a few more times—"Everest, where are you?" Her legs moved quickly under her body so that her head could remain above water.

She threw her head to the right, left, front and back, while treading the cool Chesapeake Bay looking for her love. "Everest," she screamed again. "Please tell me where you are! Don't fucking do this to me! I need you!"

Blackness took over the place, the moon only allowed her to see her hand before her eyes. The silence was deafening and unkind.

When it became apparent that Everest was not near, she called her name again. It was more to hear each syllable of her name out loud than anything else because she knew what Everest's absence meant. Death invited itself into her life once again and she wanted to die to tell it how she felt.

"Everest," she said a little louder. Except this time she used all of the power she could muster to call her name, including the energy she couldn't spare. The blood flowing down her face, due to the open wound she sustained on her scalp, made it difficult to see. How could she save another, when it was possible that she couldn't save herself?

"Everest, oh my God please don't be dead. I'm sorry! I'm so sorry I put you through this shit," she called into the shadows. "I can't take this again. I just can't—"

Suddenly there was a soft splash in the distance, which forced Mad silent. She widened her eyes as if doing so would make her hear clearer.

"Mad," Everest whispered from within the darkness. "I'm over here, but I think my arm is broken. Help me. Please."

Mad could hear light splashing some feet away but still she couldn't see her. "Are you able to move toward me? Toward my voice?"

"I can't swim to you, Mad, can you come to me? I'm in a lot of pain."

Mad's heart punched the walls of her chest, because before that moment she was resigned to the fact that she lost her forever. Just like she lost Glitter and Passion, the only other women she ever loved.

In an effort to get closer to Everest, Madjesty scrutinized her surroundings, but the darkness was unkind. Where was she? It was as shadowy out there as being submerged into a body of black ink. No light. No sight. No nothing.

"Stay right where you are," Mad suggested. "I'm coming, Everest. Just keep saying my name so that I know that I'm getting closer."

"Mad," Everest said weakly. "Mad...Mad...Mad..."

With each call of her name Mad was brought closer to her presence, until she was within Everest's breathing space. There she was...finally. The new love of her life. Under the glow of the moon Mad could see Everest's distraught face. She looked paralyzed with fear, and Mad knew she had to be strong for both of them if they were going to survive.

"I'm right here," Mad said, as her legs wagged within the water. "I fucking thought I lost you. You can't do me like that. You messed my head up just now. Do you know what I've been through? Do you have any idea what going through a loss again would do to a nigga like me?"

When Everest drifted under the water as if she was about to drown, Mad grabbed her arm to prevent her from floating away, until Everest screamed out in pain.

"No, Mad, please don't touch my arm, it hurts too badly."

Mad released her right arm and gripped at the collar of her shirt instead so that she wouldn't submerge into the water. "I'm sorry, which one is it?" She looked her over.

"My right arm. It feels like it ain't attached anymore."

Madjesty treaded in front of her, close enough to see the hazelnut color of her eyes and the sparkle of her wet braids. "Try not to move it so much, just keep treading.

Whatever you do don't stop moving your legs or you'll go under. You gotta fight, Everest."

"I don't know how much longer I can tread either, Mad." She sounded defeated. "I feel so weak, and tired. It doesn't look like I'm going to make it."

"Well float on your back instead. And I'll hold onto your shirt so that you won't drift away. Whatever you do don't give up so easily, we gonna be okay."

Everest quickly obeyed and her body popped up on the top of the water, revealing the curves of her breasts through the yellow t-shirt she was wearing. Even at her worst, Everest was still breathtaking.

"That's good, just like that." Mad gripped a small portion of her shirt, not enough to weigh her down but just enough to prevent her from washing away into the bay. "Just relax, and move your legs softly because I got you. I'm not letting you go anywhere."

Even though Everest was the focus, Mad's vitality was depleting also but she wouldn't let Everest know, because she didn't want her to worry.

"Are you gonna be okay?" Everest asked with hopefulness, as she looked into Mad's face. "Your head looks kind of bad, baby."

"Who me," she smiled, "Shit, I'm gonna be fine. I'm a soldier. You just relax because I'm worried about you."

Everest smiled believing every word. "Are *we* gonna be okay?"

"Yes, somebody's gonna find us." Mad looked out into the darkness and saw nothing and no one. "Trust me," she said less confidently.

Everest sobbed quietly as she continued to flap her legs to stay a float. "It was all worth it to me, Mad. Every painful moment of it. And if I had it to do all over again, I wouldn't hesitate for one minute."

"Do you really mean that?"

"Yes." She smiled again. "You saved me from myself the day I met you and even if we die together tonight, that will always be true."

CHAPTER 1

MAD

SIX MONTHS EARLIER

I was lying face down on the ground, with the taste of yesterday's Hennessey, cheeseburger and blood in my mouth. A pile of hock spit rested not too far from my face. An old lady threw it there as she yelled; *get a job bum*, at me about an hour earlier.

Fuck that bitch!

I fought a dude the night before who kept telling me that I stole his shoes even though he wore a size thirteen to my six in men. He hit me pretty hard in the mouth and that was the last thing I remembered before passing out.

When I raised my eyes, I could see *Tito The Bum* sitting against the brick wall some spaces away from me. I don't know him like that but we shared a bottle a few times when we came upon some dough, which was few and far between. Suddenly Tito moved closer and closer to me, like some weird 3D movie, until I could see the copper Levis button on the pocket of his blue jeans and smell the odor of feces on his skin.

Without my permission, he rubbed my red curly hair softly, and I allowed him for a minute. It was the first affection I had since I'd broken up with my ex-girlfriend Passion almost a year ago. A long story.

Every time I think about my past I get angry. My life is fucked up. *Real* fucked up. I wake up everyday with so much hate in my heart; I can feel my chest hardening. My son not in my life. My twin sister and me haven't spoken in over a year and the mother I hated died, and I never got to tell her how I felt about how she treated me to her whore face.

"It's time to get up, they kick us off this spot soon," Tito said. "You know the employees don't like to see us when they going in to work. Mothafuckas must think we gonna pull our dicks out and jerk off in their coffee or something."

He was right. I hated them and they despised me. I used the wall to stand up, and the earth felt like it was leaning sideways. I'm dizzy, tired and feel nauseous. As much as I drink I can never get use to the hangover. But being sober is worse.

When I reached into my pocket, I felt the crumpled fifty-dollar bill stuffed inside of it that I stole out of this dudes pocket last night while he was walking down the street with his hand on his girl's ass. All I needed was some liquor and I'd be okay. This world won't even matter no more.

I made my way down to the corner store and bought a half pint of Hennessey. Mr. Lin stopped giving me a hard time after I turned eighteen. He said eighteen was the new twenty-one if you had money. With about twenty something dollars left, I went to Gates Motel where I could get a room by the hour. For fifteen bucks I grabbed my room key, and the ice bucket and walked around the back of the spot to fill it up with cubes for my drink.

But when I went to get ice and saw *Wild Hair Betsy* sucking the security guard's dick by the ice machine I changed my mind. Betsy, the village prostitute, would charge the John's extra for the room without them knowing, and pocket the extra ends to score dope when she was done. She was cool though, always looked out for me when she saw police circling around the motel asking questions. And since my picture was plastered on almost every building due to a murder I didn't commit, Betsy's extra eyes came in handy.

Once I was in my room I showered, popped the top to my Hennessey and pulled the sheets back on the bed to catch a nap. But when I saw a used condom, with brown curly pubes stuck to it, I pulled the blanket back and slept on top of it instead.

While I was trying to get some sleep, thoughts of my son Cassius haunted me again. This happened every day, for every second of my life. It gets so bad sometimes that I can't look at another kid without thinking it's him. I know he'll never know who I am, and that makes it hard for me to function. I had to let my sister keep him because I'm wanted, I ain't seen him since. I don't understand why God would put this kind of pain on me and expect me to survive. Maybe my pain is his pleasure.

I dosed off after drinking the entire Hennessey bottle, but when I woke up I saw three people in my doorway. I was so tired that I didn't move, and before I knew it I drifted off to sleep again. This time when I woke up, I felt someone sitting at the foot of my bed and every time the person moved, the bed weighed down on one side and rocked.

Someone nudged my arm. "Mad, your time is up, son, we gotta go."

When I opened my eyes wider I saw Gage who was wearing her gold hoop earrings, bending down in front of me. "Come on, Mad, Betsy said some white men in suits been looking for you. You know we can't be here when it happens." Her brown skin looked red and her eyes were low like they always were when she did heroin.

Gage's real name is Lazo. Her family disowned her when she got up with Wicked, a poor white dude who also lived on the streets. When he got her pregnant years ago and she refused to leave him, the silver spoon was snatched away from her. Although she had an abortion her people ain't take her back and she was left to beat the streets with the rest of us.

It took me forever to stand up, and when I did Spirit straightened my shirt and helped me to my feet. His slanted eyes, due to his black and Chinese mix, look disappointed in me. As if I didn't feel bad enough already.

I never found out Spirit's real name. He said that in the Chinese culture a name brings with it spirits from your past good or bad. He must've been trying to leave his past behind. The only details he gave me was that he killed somebody in defense of his baby sister. So I left it alone.

"How you find me," I asked sitting back down to put on my shoes before realizing they were already on my feet. "I didn't tell nobody where I went."

Spirit rubbed his Mohawk backwards and sighed. He seemed annoyed, but so am I. "You always come here when you want to get away. We cool with that but the least you could do is tell us where you're going. We thought something happened to you."

"Yeah, we thought you got arrested," White Boy said.

White Boy, who we called WB, got skin as black as an opal stone. He hate his complexion too. Said when you are as black as he is you too dark for people to see your heart.

"You can't be bouncing on niggas without telling us where you going," WB continued.

WB, whose real name is Nathan, was raised by a white couple that adopted him shortly after moving here from Africa. When they were killed by carbon monoxide poison in their home, he was placed in the system where he said they gave him a hard time because of his skin tone. I guess he got tired of the abuse because he ran away and hit the streets with the rest of us.

"I told ya'll I'm my own person. I don't need no fucking babysitters." I grabbed my black New York Yankees baseball cap off the bed and walked toward the mirror. I looked at my face. I looked like a corpse.

"Yes you do," Gage said. "You been gone for five days, Mad. What kind of shit is that? You know they trying to find you behind that Rose Midland murder."

"I didn't kill that bitch," I yelled stepping up to her. "Wicked brought her to that fucking building and set me up. You know that."

They looked scared of me and I backed down.

"You know we believe you," she responded. "I don't know why he trying to set you up but I believe you."

"I don't know why either, that's your boy not mine!"

"We not the enemy," WB said in a low voice. "But if you don't slow down and stay low, you not gonna be able to prove your innocence."

When the door opened, Fierce was standing on the other side. Fierce was a cool black kid who was scrawny and always sickly. I don't know why but I connected with him and Spirit the most. "We gotta get out of here. I think the police roaming around out front. Come with me."

My heart dropped.

I can't go anywhere or do anything without the cops looking for me. I have to stay in hiding because I don't wanna go to jail, especially for some shit I didn't do. My life's a mess.

I slammed my cap on my head, and we all ran out of the room. I followed Fierce toward an old black Buick. "Whose car is this?"

"Something we picked up along the way," Spirit said. "Now come on, we gotta roll."

I slid into the backseat and Spirit eased on my right while Gage caught my left side.

Fierce grabbed the steering wheel of the stolen car and WB dipped into the passenger seat.

This is what my life was about these days...always on the run.

"Is Wicked there?" I asked, referring to the place I knew they were taking me.

"Yes," Gage responded. "He's there with our mother and father."

I sighed. "I thought we agreed that we wouldn't do that bamma shit anymore," I said to her.

"What shit?" Gage responded.

"Call Daze and Killer your mother and father just because you was once in their clique. If they not your blood they not your parents. So cut the dumb shit."

Gage looked at everyone else and then back at me. "You're right, Mad. From here on out that term is done." She looked at everybody else. "Agreed?"

One by one they nodded.

Although when I first met them they explained to me how they went about referring to the people in their crew, the terms mother and father was reserved for the leaders and I never took well to the terms.

"So, Mad, let me tell you what you missed while you were gone," Gage said excitedly. "You know Fortune be wearing them fake ass diamond earrings right?"

I don't respond.

"You know, the ones she be trying to pass off as real," Spirit added.

I just nodded hoping they would move the story along.

"Well anyway, we was out front of the Korean's spot last night. Spirit had some money from selling them CD's he yanked off the bootlegger out southeast and treated everybody to shrimp fried rice."

"I had the beef and broccoli, ya'll had the—"

"Spirit, shut the fuck up and stop interrupting me," Gage yelled across me at him. "You know I hate that shit when I'm telling my story."

These two were always fighting with each other. Truth be told Spirit was feeling Gage but Gage was still in love with her ex-boyfriend Wicked so she didn't notice.

"Girl, go ahead and finish," Spirit added. "You take too long to tell a story anyway."

"Like I was saying, Mad"— she rolled her eyes— "so we out front of the Korean store the other night, and Fortune was swinging her hair real hard trying to show us that she can move like Beyoncé and shit. When one of the earrings popped out of her ear, Gypsy, the store's dog, ate the mothafucka"— Gage broke out laughing but I didn't catch the joke — "she tried everything to get this earring back from this dog including opening his jaws. She acted like the thing was real."

"That mothafucka almost bit her hand off too," WB laughed as he lit a blunt.

"So when she couldn't get it out, please tell me why she kidnapped the dog later on that night and fed him all these laxatives that she stole from the pharmacy? She was up all night feeding the dog pills like they were candy and shit. It was so sad."

"She had the dog in her cubby and everything, my nigga," Fierce laughed taking the blunt from WB. "Fortune was on a mission."

"The dog shitted on everything in her room," Gage continued. "Man, I'm talking about wet shit, the kind that smells so bad it don't clean up even after you wash it. You know Nic who lives across from Spirit?" she paused. "Well anyway he got mad cause the dog broke down his door and shitted on his pillow. Nic thinks it was done on purpose, you know he be on his conspiracy shit, but I think the dog was dehydrated and tired and just ended up in there."

"Nic is fucking crazy," WB said in a low voice. "Always thinking a nigga out to get him."

"The thing is all that shitting and she still didn't get the earing out of the dog's ass," Spirit added.

"So then she tries to take the dog back to the Korean's but now it won't go away. She drops the dog off but when she gets back, he's right in front of her cubby...shitting. Man, she tried beating him, yelling at him and everything but nothing worked. I think it fucks with her now or something. I just..."

I zoned out of the conversation at this point. I knew what she was doing. They did this type of thing all the time when I was down. They usually did it on the days I would wake up silent with nothing to say. Even though I would sometimes go five days without talking, I never woke up and said today is the day I'm going to be mute. I just didn't have it in my heart to speak. And no matter how hard they tried they would never understand who I am and the hate I feel inside.

"...So it was so crazy," Gage continued, as if I heard everything else she said.

Before long, since I ain't respond, they abandoned their show and left me to my silence. I liked it better this way. That's how I knew they were true friends because they could sit with me in silence even if they didn't want to.

After driving for a while, when we made a left and then a right, I knew we were close to the place I was becoming too familiar with. The place I left because the dude Wicked, who also lives here, makes me wanna kill him.

Fierce stashed the car around the corner, Spirit and Gage wiped off our fingerprints and we ditched the stolen ride. When we were done we walked toward the DuPont Circle tunnel, which use to be home to underground trolleys. Now its full of dust, rats and people like us.

The moment we reached the East Wing's entrance, I was met by *Old Man Young*. Dirt and his gray hair took over so much of his face that the only thing you could see was his piercing blue eyes. He never went anywhere without his long and dusty green trench coat, which stank of piss and cigarettes.

He smiled, revealing his black teeth.

"Hello, Mad, welcome back to The Catacombs."

CHAPTER 2
MAD

When I walked back into The Catacombs I felt hopeless. First let me say that living in The Catacombs ain't no luxurious experience. It takes a lot of getting use to and a life so terrible that being here is your last option, and unfortunately for me both situations apply.

Let me give you a little history on myself. I was born to a whore named Harmony Phillips about twenty-something years ago, and spent most of my life believing I was a boy. I didn't believe it because it was something I imagined. My fucked up mother told me I was a dude. It wasn't until I caught my period in class while writing on the blackboard that I learned I was something else - although to this day I disagree. In my heart I'm all man.

I was born a twin, but my sister and me disconnected shortly after my mother moved us to Washington DC from Texas - that's another long story. When I was growing up it was nothing to see roaches, rats and spiders in my bedroom. My mother didn't keep a clean house and she didn't buy supplies for my sister and me to clean up neither. The toilets were always backed up, forcing us to pee on piles of dirty clothes in our room. If number two hit us, we would grab a dirty pot out of the kitchen sink, shit in it and dump it in the backyard. The reason the toilet stayed stopped up was because of the amount of used condoms my mother use to flush down it.

So I got some experience living in fucked up conditions if you know what I mean. Still, nothing I experienced in my life could prepare me for this shit right here.

When you walk into The Catacombs the first thing that hits you is complete darkness. I'm talking about blackness so deep you can't feel your own body. It's like you're floating in outer space, with no walls or ground, and you're immediately dizzy. If you don't belong here, unless you're just crazy of course, you'll turn around and run. But the residents who do live here know that just a few feet up from the entrance, on the left, are flashlights stashed behind three large grey cinder blocks. We use them to brighten up the pathway leading deeper into the tunnel.

Going a little further inside, down the middle of The Catacombs, are trolley tracks that Old Man Young said were used about a hundred years ago to transport people in and around Washington DC. Now they are just in the way, and make it difficult to walk in the darkness for the people who live here.

Everywhere you step there are large piles of cinder blocks, that if you aren't careful, you can trip and twist your ankle like Fierce did a year back, when he was running from a pack of stray dogs who were trying to kill him. He was down a whole week, and needed people to help him do everything, including walk to the Shit Pot, which I'll explain later.

If you still want to push forward after the darkness, trolley tracks and cinder block traps, then you better be ready to deal with the smell. This is what usually keeps outsiders away because the odor is so strong it burns the hairs of your nostrils and never goes away. Before they brought me here, Gage tried to describe the scent to me. She said it was a cross between shit, piss, rotten fish and mold cooked in a cast iron pot, with a gallon of chitterlings soaking inside.

If The Catacombs' perfume doesn't make you jet then maybe the human size rats that feel they have just as much right to be here as you will do the trick. They'll steal your food, chew your skin and if you let them, give you dirty diseases that will kill you in the middle of the night, like they did to Miranda's baby when he was sleeping one night. The baby died because the rats ate him to death.

Once you get past the front entrance things get a little more organized. The Catacombs is shaped like a big plus sign with four different wings—the East, West, North and South. Spirit manages the East Wing, where everyone walks through to enter The Catacombs. That's where I live, with about twenty-two other people.

We got rules in our wing, which limits the amount of problems we run into. For instance all cubby holes, which some call apartments, have steel meshes at the doorways that you have to step over to get inside of your place. It's a little irritating when it snags onto your shoes, but it keeps rats from bothering you like in other wings. The only thing you have to do is dispose of all food at night or else.

Each cubby is made out of any material you can find, and connected to the wall of the tunnel. The doors are usually made up of cardboard and the threat of bodily harm is enough to keep other residents out of your space, instead of locks.

Now on the opposite side of us, way down the other side of The Catacombs is the West Wing. About thirty something people live there. On that end of The Catacombs anything goes. Fighting happens at all hours of the night, people die for no reason, and it's so dirty that everyone who lives down there has an extra odor to their bodies, in addition to the one that's already in the tunnel. You can smell a West Winger coming because they don't do anything to stay clean.

Although Spirit gets mad at the residents in the West, because of how they keep their hall, they still leave food all over the place. Half of the rats in the tunnel are because of them. Wicked, whom I despise, is in charge of the madness over there so shit ain't never right.

Standing at the end of the East Wing, also known as The Crossroad, is where all of the wings connect. There are two light posts that extend above the ground where a father and son team we call Engineer One and Engineer Two, (nicknamed E1 and E2 for short), tap the power lines so we can have lights in our cubbies when the streetlights come on. All of the power leading into the cubbies inside of The Catacombs was stolen and set up by them. Without lights I wouldn't be here.

Standing at The Crossroads, if you look straight ahead you'll be facing the West Wing. If I walk left I'll be in the South Wing, also known as The Shit Pot, which is the place where residents use the bathroom and dump it after their done in holes within the ground. I never go down there though, I hold mine until I can't stand it no more, and then I use the bathroom at Lenny's Restaurant a few blocks up the street, outside of The Catacombs. Besides, the smell in the Shit Pot is so strong that if I do gotta go I can't because the only thing I can think about is the smell.

If I look to my right in The Crossroads, that's the North Wing, but no one lives there. Now if you keep walking in the North Wing, until you can't go no more, you'll be outside. You can't get into The Catacombs this way from the North Wing, because trees and a narrow pathway, which is blocked by a green flatbed crane dump truck, surround it. So we kind of feel safe out there. We call this area The Pit, which is where we light fires in trash cans, talk shit, and try to make sense of our world. The dump truck sits a little ways out and has a truck bed where some people go to have sex if they got somebody willing.

So that's my world now. It's where I ended up. The crazy thing is if you can get past all of the grossness something strange happens. Old Man Young said its like people who know they going to die and make peace with it. He says once you know you're going to die the horror in it is gone. It's just like The Catacombs. Once you know this is all you got left, and nobody else wants you, you deal with it and get on with life.

I was standing in the doorway of Spirit's cubby in the East Wing, where everybody who's family hangs out. He got a bed made out of an old couch, straight ahead against the wall, and a long seat that he made by stapling pillows on a slab of wood, to the right. He also has lots of fold up chairs for his guests and a red rug with black writing that says *Yin and Yang* that sits in the middle of the floor. At least five candles are burning at any given time and the smell is so sweet you almost forget where you are. *Almost.* To the left are a bunch of cords running from outside of his cubby, leading to a small fridge. Beside it is a table, with a hot plate, and paper cups that he uses if he has food, which we rarely do.

I walked inside and sat on the long seat against the wall. Gage sat next to me, and WB and Fierce grabbed chairs and sat in the middle of the cubby.

Spirit walked inside, stood in front of us and said, "We gotta find something to eat. Anybody got any money on them?"

Since I already spent most of my fifty on a bottle and the room I stayed quiet.

"Naw, but I got some CD's I'm gonna try and move later on tonight, maybe I can get something then," WB responded rubbing his dark brown heroin track ridden arms.

"What about you," he asked Fierce.

"No, I don't have nothing either."

"What about you, Gage?"

"I'm out too, Spirit," she said. "Sorry."

As she sat next to me she rubbed her leg against mine. I think Spirit caught it because his expression went from business mode to kind of sad. WB told me that Gage was feeling me but I hoped it wasn't the case because I'm not feeling her at all. That's the last thing I'm thinking about so I moved a few inches away from her.

"It's been a rough month," she continued, "we gonna have to find a better way to get our paper around here or we die."

Although I been gone, I dug into my pocket and pulled out the few bucks I had and slammed them onto the floor by my feet. "Ya'll can have that. It's all I got left." I pulled my cap down over my eyes.

"Mad, we ain't talking about you," Spirit told me. "You haven't even been here."

I left the money anyway. I don't need it because I'm not hungry and it ain't enough to buy a bottle.

"You so fucking sweet," Gage said rubbing my leg again. "You always looking out for us. I'm gonna start looking out for you too."

I moved away from her again, and everybody pretended not to see it by turning away. Gage was bugging out.

"Hey, I wanted to talk to Gage for a second," Wicked said entering Spirit's place with a small paper bag in his hand. He looked at Gage who was sitting next to me before his eyes stopped on my face. "So when did you get back?" he asked me.

His friends Daze and his girlfriend Killer were behind him.

I didn't respond. I have no words for the white boy. Gage's pale skin reddened and his grey eyes stared directly into mine.

"So you not gonna answer me?" he stepped into the cubby. "You had my friends everywhere looking for you and you not going to answer me? What the fuck is up with you bouncing every time you get an attitude? Either you with us or you not."

As bad as I wanted to tell him where to go I remained silent.

"Just leave it alone, Wicked," Spirit said. "He back now so let it go."

Wicked sighed. "Why do ya'll keep referring to this chick as a he? She ain't no fucking he, she's a bitch."

I knew what he was trying to do but he could do it alone. It was because of Wicked my life was on the lam anyway. Had he not brought this chick into this abandoned warehouse where I went to with Spirit and the gang one night when I first met them, and had she not gotten killed, I wouldn't be on the run now. The thing that got to Wicked more than anything though was that Spirit, Gage, WB, and Fierce all took my side, even though they'd just met me at that point.

Although I wasn't scared of him, I also knew The Catacombs had rules. And one of them was no fighting or stealing from another because you could be voted out. And since I had no place else to go my hands were tied.

"What do you want anyway," WB asked Wicked interrupting his gaze on me. "You came in here for a reason."

He rubbed his baldhead, gave me another look and said, "Like I said I want to talk to Gage alone."

"I don't want to talk to you, Wicked," she sighed. She stood up and walked away from him. "I told you that when you asked me earlier."

"Gage, you can't keep ignoring me and shit," he yelled. "How much longer do you think I'm gonna take it before I snap? We were together for years. The least you can do is hear me out. It's been months and you still mad over some dead bitch I fucked once."

"That's just it, you think that's okay, and that's why I'm done with you," she responded. "Anyway I don't love you no more. Move on Wicked. I have."

Wicked grabbed his dick. "Gage, you gonna make me blow."

"Just leave her alone," Spirit yelled.

Wicked laughed. "So you think just cause I'm not fucking her no more that she'll want you? She'll never want you, slim. She had a real man when I was with her and she will never forget it. Besides you too weak."

"She don't want to talk, Wicked, so bounce," I finally said while still sitting in my seat.

He looked down at me and I stood up. We were staring directly into each other's eyes.

"Wicked, let's go," Daze, who was nicknamed for his constant high appearance said as he stood in the doorway. "She doesn't want to talk."

Daze was the leader of The Catacombs, until everyone divided after Rose Midland was murdered. Some people blamed Wicked and some blamed me. Those who took Wicked's side moved to the West Wing, and those who stood by me stayed in The East.

When Wicked didn't move Daze and Killer pulled him softly by the hand until he snatched away from them. Daze's dark skin was gray, from all of the heroin he shot up. And Killer's light skin was starting to look brown from all of the dope she did.

"Give me a second," Wicked said. He looked at me and said, "I'm sorry I came at you like that, Mad. I mean, you don't understand, these were my friends before the stuff at the building tore us apart."

His apology was so fake it didn't warrant a response.

"Anyway, I miss ya'll," Wicked said to them. "I would give my life for each one of you. I was hoping that we could start all over, if ya'll wanted to."

Wicked wanted power and he was willing to do anything he could to get it.

"I'm gonna be honest, we not feeling that right now, Wicked," WB said cracking his knuckles. "You gotta check us later on the reconciliation thing."

He frowned. "It's been almost a year. How much longer you gonna hold that shit against me? I made a mistake by bringing the girl to the building. But how was I to know that she was going to be murdered and Mad was going to be framed for it?"

As he hung in the doorway, Nic from across the way pushed metal slabs and a few bags of groceries in his shopping cart toward his cubby. Now everybody was focused on him instead of Wicked.

"I'm letting everybody know right now that they better not come in my cubby for shit," he yelled with a screw face. "I'm gonna stay to myself for now, just like the fuck ya'll better stay to your own. Got that dog shitting in my cubby. Thinking shit is a joke. Stay the fuck away from me. All of you!"

We all walked out of Spirit's cubby and stared at Nic. "Fuck is wrong with you, Nic?" Spirit asked.

"You know what the fuck is wrong. Every time I needed something all ya'll did was look out for each other and ignore me. Nobody ever bothered to stop me and ask me if I wanted a drink, or something to eat. But now I got a job and I don't need nobody.

"You better be careful." Wicked said. He looked like he wanted to murder him. "You pushing your luck."

"Fuck luck! Look where we live! In a tomb!"

Nic was always bringing up shit niggas forgot about months ago. Like the time he asked Gage if he could fuck her in The Dump, and she slapped him in the eye. Whenever he would see her after that he would say, "That wasn't right that you slapped me, Gage. Wasn't right at all." He promised to get back at her, which is why she never walked anywhere in The Catacombs without one of us.

Then there was the time Nic was playing Chess with Old Man Young, and Fierce accidently knocked the board over when he was watching the game due to having a seizure. Although they picked up the pieces after the seizure, and agreed on where the pieces went before playing, Nic still blamed both of them when he lost. Since the game was being played for beer, he swore Old Man Young and Fierce were in cahoots and promised to get back at them.

He did too because a few days later, somebody put piss in Old Man Young's chili that he was making in his crock-pot and Fierce couldn't find his inhaler, after suffering a serious asthma attack. Everybody knew Nic was involved but figured if they just ignored him, he'd go away. But he never did.

Nic stayed up all night hammering into the walls and building his wooden and metal doors that he promised. If he had so much money I don't understand why he wouldn't just leave and get a real apartment up top. It wasn't like we wanted him here anyway. Maybe he was institutionalized like Old Man Young said happened to prisoners after being in jail so long. Maybe leaving The Catacombs wasn't in him.

Later on that night I was sleeping in the makeshift bed in Gage's cubby in the East Wing when I realized I was sweating. I stayed with her because when she broke up with Wicked a year back, she had the extra space for me. When I smelled the strong scent of cooked meat and smoke I hopped up.

"Gage, get up," I said pushing her arm roughly. She was in her bed, still asleep. I coughed a few times to clear my lungs. "Get the fuck up, something is wrong!"

"What's going on?" she asked me. She hacked a few times too.

"I think something is on fire. Let's get the fuck out of here."

When we rushed out of the cubby and looked down, we heard screaming and yelling throughout the tunnel. Down the way, through the smoke, I saw Spirit standing in the front of Nic's cubby and I wondered what was up. It wasn't until I rushed up to the scene that I learned what was happening.

"What's going on?" I asked Spirit, as I coughed some more.

"Somebody set Nic on fire. I think he may be dead."

CHAPTER 3
WICKED

Wicked stomped into his cubby in the West Wing with Daze and Killer following him. After Wicked murdered Nic by dousing his cubby with lighter fluid and throwing a match, Daze caught up with him and forced him down to the West Wing.

"What the fuck is wrong with you?" Daze yelled approaching Wicked. "Do you realize you just killed a member of The Catacombs, which goes against the law down here? You could be forced out. Is that what you want?"

"You don't understand," Wicked said pacing the small place in front of him. "He kept fucking with us, and kept taunting me"— he rubbed his baldhead roughly— "didn't you hear him? I mean if he had a job and money why he wanna stay down here? Why not go up top and live with them?"

Killer, in a soft voice, approached Wicked. "We all know that, that isn't the reason you killed him," she said. "You killed him because you're angry with Mad. But I'm here to say that you're playing yourself."

Wicked's eyes lowered. "And if I did do it because that bitch fucked with my head so what?"

"That's not the way you handle things, Wicked," she responded. "You know you can't survive up top. You have too many things on your police record just like we do. You want federal time?"

"But why does she have to be here?" Wicked yelled, throwing his hands up in the air. He acted like a spoiled brat instead of a twenty something year old man. "And why is Gage, WB, Fierce and Spirit always taking her side?"— He placed his hand over his heart— "After all of the things I did for them? It was me who got the medicines when Fierce had his asthma attacks, seizures and strokes. Me, not that dyke"— he beat his chest— "I risked my life robbing them pharmacies. And this is how they pay me? With disloyalty? I run this fucking group and its high time I remind them!"

Daze stepped back after Wicked's proclamation. Because although it was widely whispered that Wicked was really in charge of their small network of friends, everyone knew that Daze was officially supposed to be in charge.

"I run this group, Wicked," Daze said firmly. "Not you!"

"Well run it then," he responded walking away. He slumped down on the only gray chair in his room, and placed his face in his hands. "I just...I just don't know anymore what's going on with us. I want Gage to understand I made a mistake. That's all."

Daze tried to bite his tongue but the disrespect he felt at the moment for his friend was blinding him. So his girlfriend, always the faithful chick, stepped up.

"If you want Mad gone you have to take another approach," Killer said rubbing Wicked's head softly. "You don't make her out to be a martyr by fussing at her every chance you get. She has a hot temper. Help her hang herself."

"But what about Gage? I was with her for years, and now she won't even talk to me. It's like Mad got her hypnotized. It's like she has all of them hypnotized, and I can't get through to them."

"You need to let Gage go," Killer responded.

"I will never let her go," he yelled. "Do you hear me?" His response was so intense that both of them backed up.

"Then act like you've let her go at least," Daze responded. "Show interest in someone else in The Catacombs. If Gage is really for you, she'll come around."

"You really think so?"

"Unless you think Mad is competition," Killer said slyly.

"That chick still ain't no competition for me," Wicked replied. "I don't care what rubber dick she wearing between her legs."

"Well then prove it," Daze added. "Back off and let Gage come to you."

CHAPTER 4
MAD

Me, Spirit, Gage and WB were sitting on a couch with no cushion in Old Man Young's cubby. He slept on the couch at night, but preferred to sit on pillows on the floor like he was now. His crib wasn't the most comfortable place to be, but that wasn't why people came. He knew how to tell a fucking story.

Since Nic died somebody stole a package of dope out of Spirit's cubicle, and the gang was trying to cheer him up.

WB sold his CD's to make it nice so he bought us a pizza, and Old Man Young a cheese steak and a Pepsi. For a sandwich he would tell some of the best stories you ever heard in your life, better than anything you could ever see or hear on TV. None of us had been to sleep after Nic was set on fire, so we needed this. Although niggas were mums the word about the burning, most of us knew who lit the match—Wicked. But there was no use in pointing fingers either. Truth was The Catacombs was better with Nic gone anyway, but I couldn't help but wonder if Wicked thought he was more powerful now since he wasn't challenged and got away with it. Even down this nasty mothafucka there are politics.

After we scraped Nic's burnt body out of his cubby, we took him out North exit to The Pit. I can't give you a count, but I know a lot of members from The Catacombs were buried there. It's the only way to get rid of bodies, unless you want the cops coming down here asking questions. We handle our own dead. But lately even outside of Nic, strange bodies had been ending up in The Catacombs. Who were they? Where did they come from? Maybe Wicked was doing that shit too.

Sitting Indian style on the floor after eating his sandwich Old Man Young said, "I use to deal with this woman in Spartanburg, South Carolina."

That's how he started all of his stories. No introduction or anything. He just got straight down to it.

"She was as small as a pole with no muscles anywhere on her body. She didn't have a single tooth in her mouth either. She would eat big meals and throw up in the toilet or out of her bathroom window, thinking I didn't know about it. Breath reeked higher than all of the West Wingers put together. Well one day..."

I didn't hear him anymore because Gage was running her hand up the middle of my back. Her warm fingers traveled along the grooves of my muscles, and I stood up because she was making me want to fuck.

Gage was a good person, the kind of person you liked to be around because she's always looking out for your well being. But, I don't look at her like that. I never have, and never will. It seemed like sooner or later one of my friends were always trying to fuck me.

Sugar, who was a good friend of mine back in the day, wanted something from me I couldn't give her either. The foulest part is that she was the one who told me my mother died and I never got to tell her how pretty she looked. Or how happy I was for her and my homie Krazy K who she eventually got up with. I never saw her again. I'm not gonna make the same mistake by making Gage think that there can be anything else between us.

"Why you standing up?" Fierce asked me after coughing a few times. He was always sick but I guess living down here ain't good for nobody's lungs.

I reached into my pocket and handed Fierce his inhaler. He never carried it and I always worried about him so I held onto it for him when I wasn't drunk or could remember.

"Thanks, man," he said taking a pull. "But where you going?"

"I'm about to go out to The Pit"— I looked down at Gage who was smiling up at me— "I'll be back."

"But you never leave on one of Old Man Young's stories," Spirit said. "You once said he was the highlight of The Catacombs. What you got an extra bottle on you or something?"

"Come on, son," I told him. "If I got something ya'll got something too. You know that."

"True," Gage said, standing up. "Well if you're leaving we're coming with you."

I tried to hide my irritation, but sometimes you just want to be alone. I got the impression that they thought by playing me close, I wouldn't walk out of the tunnel. I can tell they really don't know me that well. Because when I'm ready to bounce there won't be shit anybody could do to stop me.

"You youngins go on ahead," Old Man Young said to them. "I want to talk to Mad alone for a minute." They all walked out of the cub, and for some reason he laid into me like he was my father. "You got a lot of work to do, Mad."

I frowned. "Fuck you talking about?"

I bent down and brushed the piece of dirt that popped up on my sneakers. Maybe out of nervousness. I hated when people said they wanted to talk to me. Although I live down here, there will be one thing that always stays fresh on me, and that's my shoes.

"You are misguided right now, Mad." He stood up.

"If you talking about the back rubbing thing you gotta rap to Gage, because that was all her and not me."

"I'm not talking about Gage. What I'm talking about is much deeper, young man. You don't belong here, and you gotta leave and find out what's holding you back from your destiny."

"How you come out the blue and talk to me 'bout my life? You don't know shit about me. I barely even talk to people in here 'bout my life. And if I do get to talking you won't be in the room."

"I've been around a long time. I'm just giving you my advice. If you don't take it now you're going to need it later. So you should respect me."

I laughed. "Why I gotta respect you? Just cause you old? All my life the only thing older people did was give me a hard time. Now you good with the stories and all. But you better stick to the stories about your *own* life and leave mine out of it."

I walked out.

●━━━━━━━━━━━━━━━━━━━━━━━━━━━●

The fire in The Pit was extra hot tonight, and caused my face to moisten. Spirit was talking to Fierce about fucking some chick out West and I knew he was lying so I thought the shit was funny. With all the liquor and the good convo flowing around The Pit, the only thing I was thinking about was Cassius and what Old Man Young said about not belonging here. I wanted to be with my son more than I wanted anything else in the world, but it's out of my hands right now. I'm wanted for murder.

As I watched Fierce who didn't look well walk away Gage approached me. "Why do you keep fighting me?" she was drunk off of the cheap vodka that was floating around.

"I'm not fighting you," I said stepping away a little.

"You hate me don't you," Gage said sadly. She only had one earring on, and she was going to be mad as hell in the morning if she couldn't find the other hoop.

I continued to look into the fire. "How can I be mad at you? You didn't do shit to me."

"Your name is Mad," she giggled, "so it should be easy for you to be angry. Come on. Stop fighting. All I'm trying to do is get to know you."

"All you trying to do is get your mind off of Wicked by using me. I'm not second prize. I fuck with you tough shawty but that ain't me."

She exhaled so hard it looked as if she was about to blow the fire out. "What the fuck is wrong with me?"

Damn I wish she would sit her drunk ass down somewhere.

"Look, I'm sorry about earlier," she continued. "You know, when I put my hand on you at Old Man Young's. But you looked like you had something on your mind, and I wanted to cheer you up a little. If you let me I can make your entire body tremble."

I could tell now that she wasn't going to let it go so I had to cut deep. "I'm not interested in you, Gage." I looked into her eyes so that she would know I was serious. "I wanna put that out there so there won't be no confusion. I been in and out of relationships all my life, and it ain't for me no more. I hope you understand."

At first she seemed angry but then she looked at me as if she wanted to lick me clean. "We can fuck in secret," she said biting her bottom lip. "I know you think about sex all the time. If you don't that's crazy because everybody in The Catacombs sure does. Why you think The Dump always be occupied? It's the only thing we can do around here to take our mind off of our troubles."

"Even if I wanted to go there with you I would never do it in The Dump. I ain't never been that pressed to fuck."

"Yes you would."

"Never." I repeated.

"Never say never," she said winking. "You'd do it especially if I was Everest."

I never met Everest but she already got on my nerves. They acted like she was God. She'd been gone for two years and everybody claimed she was out seeing the world.

Gage rubbed my arm again. "Come on, Mad. Fuck me like you want to." She rubbed her hand over her pussy. "I can see in your eyes you want some of this."

I'ma be honest, I got a lot of things running through my mind right now. Yes I wouldn't mind getting my shit off. Like I said, Gage is a pretty girl. But, the truth is I'm the only one in here who washes at the carry out up the street. The rest of them use water in buckets at The Crossroads. That ain't good enough for me. I never smelled Gage's pussy, don't get me wrong, but I'm not feeling sex with her either.

"Mad, please fuck me. I want you so badly."

I looked at her pretty eyes and wet pink lips. I tried not to focus on her breasts, but they look good too. I can't remember the last time I been with a woman, and I can't predict when it will happen again. When I remembered that she was drunk and this was wrong because Spirit was next in line to be with her I pulled myself together.

"You want me to leave The Catacombs? And find a place up top to go?"

She immediately looked confused. "No...what are you talking about?"

"Because you pushing me, and I don't like to be pushed, Gage. If you want me to hang around here, you can't keep backing me in no corners. I don't like that shit."

Her head lowered. "I understand."

"I'm serious."

"I get it...I just," her voice dropped lower, "never mind."

We continued to look into the fire in silence, until Wicked came into The Pit with his arm around Speedstar's neck. Speedstar rolled with a group called *The Little Liars* from the West Wing, and I wondered when they got together. As far as I knew Speedstar used to be cool with Gage. Speedstar was a cute black girl with tattoos all over her body and face, and to be honest if she didn't live in The West I could see myself fucking her too.

"Why it's so dead out here?" Wicked asked nobody in particular. He slobbed Speedstar down before looking at Gage and then at me. He was obviously trying to make Gage jealous. "Lately ya'll been acting dead and shit. Do something, Mad. Entertain me."

I didn't respond. The nigga's a clown who's doing a good job of entertaining himself.

"Why you looking like you wanna fight?" Wicked asked looking my way. "You wanna fight me or something, Mad? You wanna prove to everybody in The Catacombs that you a real man?"

"Leave her alone," Gage yelled. Her fists were balled up so I could tell she wanted to hit him or Speedstar.

"Oh...now she's a girl. I thought she was a dude. Which one is it going to be, Mad? Are you a bitch or a nigga? I mean make up your fucking mind."

I still don't respond.

"I get it. You wanna act like I'm not here all of a sudden. Well one day you gonna talk to me," he continued. "One day real soon too."

When Fierce started coughing loudly, I rushed over to him. I didn't even see him come back to The Pit. "You aight, man?" I asked him.

"Yeah...I gotta go get my inhaler. It's in my cubby. I'll be back."

"You want me to come with you?" I asked.

"No...go back. I'm fine."

As I watched him walk down the hall, I saw Fish from the East Wing running up to the entrance of The Pit. He looked worried.

"Mad, whatever you do stay out here. Some people asking for you at the entrance to The Catacombs dressed in navy blue suits. I think they may be cops."

CHAPTER 5

MAD

I'm still at The Pit not understanding how the police found me at The Catacombs. And if they knew I was here, why didn't they come in with guns blazing to take me out? After all, according to the world, I killed Rose Midland.

"What exactly did they look like?" Gage asked Fish. She looked more worried than me. "Did they say they were coming back?"

Fish was an East Winger who had come to The Catacombs about two years before me. Sometimes they called him the Gatekeeper, because he loved being by himself and would hang out front near the entrance. He did anything he could to pass time. From spraying graffiti on the walls, to bashing rocks until they turned to sand. He got a long black face with huge big lips and I think that's why he picked the name Fish.

"They look like two white men," he said apparently still nervous. "They gave me the spooks though. I don't got a good feeling, Mad."

He kept looking behind him and that made me even more noid. We don't do well with people who don't belong here coming into our space. There are people who live here who are in more trouble than what I want to know about. You come here if it's your last choice, not your first.

"You better be easy, Mad," Wicked said, with his arm still wrapped around Speedstar's neck. He had a sly look on his face. He loved this shit. "You don't wanna be out on them streets and get yourself locked up now do you? The last thing we want is for something to happen to you. I know your little crew over there would be devastated."

"Why don't you just shut the fuck up, Wicked," Gage said as she tossed a rock into the fire. "Always starting shit. Besides, it's your fault she's in this to begin with."

****

What Happened The Night Rose Was Murdered
****

We were in an abandoned building that they nick-named 'The Hole' in Washington, D.C. They hung out there before they met me. Me, Gage and Spirit just cracked opened a bottle of Hennessy when Wicked, White Boy, Fierce, Daze and Killer walked in with a white girl who seemed out of place. She had red hair and was wearing a white dress that looked like she just left the prom. Her name was Rose Midland.

A little dizzy, I used the wall to stand up and readied myself to greet the squad. Wicked and his crew embraced Gage and Spirit without acknowledging me at first.

When they were done Spirit said, "Wicked, I want you to meet one of the realest niggas I know." He walked him over to me and I reached out to shake his hand. He didn't accept and I knew right away I didn't like him.

Wicked with his dark gray eyes looked at me and said, "Cool tat." He pointed at my arm. "Who's Cassius?"

"My son." I looked down at the tattoo, which read 'Cassius Phillips Lost But Soon Found'.

"That's hot." He didn't ask more questions about my son. "I heard it's because of you we had money to help our friend." Wicked pulled over another kid who was very scrawny and sickly looking. "This man right here." He tapped him on the back. "Fierce, say hi to the person responsible for saving your life."

Fierce seemed shy but he managed a, "Hi," along with a weak wave. He looked timid and I liked him.

"What it is," I said waiting for the rest of the introductions. I pulled my cap down over my eyes.

Spirit took over the introductions. "This is White Boy," when a black kid as dark as an Opal Stone stepped up I was thrown off by his nickname. "But we call him WB."

"Don't worry about it, buddy." WB laughed I guess picking up on my facial expression. "I get that most times when people meet me. Since I'm extra dark and I tell people my name is White Boy, I always throw them off." His energy was smooth and I liked him too.

"Now this is our father, Daze." Spirit continued. A black teenager stepped up and he looked a little older than everybody else. I wondered why he referred to him as his father.

"Welcome," he said to me although I didn't believe he meant it. He didn't want me here. "This is the mother of our family, her name is Killer." Killer was a beautiful light skin girl with heroin tracks up and down her body...not just her arms. "She's the love of my life," and he pointed a stiff finger into my chest, "and she's off limits."

I stepped back not doing well with niggas touching me. After the intros all of them hung against the walls at first *and observed me. I sipped some Hennessey until I saw Gage's sad expression. I followed her stare. She was focused on her boyfriend Wicked who was enjoying Rose's attention. He disrespected Gage right to her face.*

"Who's the white girl?" Spirit asked Wicked. "She hasn't been introduced yet." Wicked's arm hung over Rose's neck and he whispered in her ear.

"My bad," he said with a smile, "we found this beauty at the train station on the way back. She was alone and crying after her fiancé' stood her up at the alter. We took a vote and everybody agrees. We like her so we'll keep her."

Gage stood behind me and I heard her crying softly. Wicked acted like Gage wasn't even his girl. Not caring about his girlfriend's (Gage) feelings he clapped his hands together. "Since we got the formalities out the way, let's party."

An hour later there was weed, liquor and other drugs circling around The Hole. Everybody seemed lighter and I felt like I was in a different world. They told me that they only used the building on certain days because the police usually ran them out every chance they got. When I asked where they go during the times they can't stay there, Spirit's response threw me off.

"Underground. We call it The Catacombs."

After awhile we all drifted off to sleep. When I woke up my head was banging. When I looked around I saw everybody was still asleep. Since I didn't know where the bathroom was I grabbed my Jordans and placed them on. Once on my feet I saw the white girl with the red hair lying on the floor, with blood all over her dress and face. Her legs were wide open along with her eyes. My heart rocked in my chest. The white bitch was dead.

"*Spirit*," *I said in a low voice. He didn't move. "Yo, Spirit, get the fuck up!" I yelled louder.*

He finally shifted and when he did, I pointed in the direction of the girl. "What the fuck!" he said scrambling to get off the floor.

His response woke up everyone else and they all screamed after seeing Rose's stiff body and bloody red hair. Daze walked up to her, placed his hand on her neck and said what we already knew. "She's not breathing." He looked at all of us and shook his head but then his eyes rested back on me.

Wicked walked slowly into my direction and said, "What's that on your shirt?"

"What?" I looked down and I saw blood all over my hands and clothes. "Wait a minute..." I didn't know what was happening. Why was her blood on my clothes? I didn't even talk to her.

"What you do to her, man?" Wicked looked like he wanted to hit me.

"I...I don't know." I wasn't even interested in her.

"What do you mean you don't know?" He persisted. "She's dead and you have blood all over your clothes."

Because I couldn't remember I assumed I went into the Drunk Zone again.

I was about to step to Wicked for thinking it was a joke that the cops were after me, when WB and Fortune came into The Pit with a bag full of groceries. Everybody's eyes lit up because this kind of thing was golden around here, and hardly ever happened. At the most somebody in my crew may luck up on a chicken box, which would be split with the closest friends, but this was different.

The dog Fortune didn't want, who swallowed her earring was right behind her. She re-named him *Leave Me Alone*. It was a yellow lab with fluffy ears and a puffy tail.

"Hear ye, hear ye, WB and Fortune have come through once again," WB yelled making an entrance. He walked up to the pit. "I got hot dogs"— he handed the pack to Gage— "I got ground beef"— he handed the pack to Spirit— "and I got rolls." He looked at my face and I wasn't smiling. "Wait a minute, why everybody out here look pissed?"

I stared at Wicked and said, "No reason."

"Yeah it ain't 'bout shit," Gage added, I guess trying to take the attention off of me and Wicked's recent beef. "Damn, WB, how you come up on all of this food?" Gage smiled and licked her lips.

"Let me tell you so you can take notes," he grinned.

"Nigga, shut up and tell the story," Gage added.

"So we were out at the grocery store trying to make some money by helping people take groceries to the car right?"

WB handed the bag to another member in The Catacombs, who placed the cooking grid over the fire blasting out of the trashcan. So that we could get the meat cooking.

"This old man had his eyes glued on Fortune's ass while she was bending over," WB continued. "So while he was looking at her, I saw his bags sitting in the cart alone. While I watched him watch her, I took his shit and split. He tried to catch me, Mad but I was gone." He laughed harder. "You know can't nobody fuck with my running game. I'm from Nigeria," he said in his native accent. "And his loss was our dinner."

The game he ran reminds me of when my mother use to make my twin sister and me steal groceries from people who parked their full grocery carts while they walked away to get their cars.

"I might have to break you off behind this, WB," Gage said.

"Don't make me fuck you up, girl," Fortune responded.

"Girl, I'm just playing with him. Dang!" She shook her head. "I'll help get these on the grill."

Gage is horny as fuck.

When the food was sitting on the grid, WB walked over to me. "I heard the cops came here earlier, man," he looked me over. "You okay?"

I sighed, and pulled my cap down. "Yeah, man, I guess I should probably leave The Catacombs huh? Since they already know where I am. I mean, what's to stop them from coming up in this bitch? WB, I'm not trying to go to jail."

"Believe it or not you safer here than you are up top. If I were you, I'd stay put. Think about it, if they weren't scared they would've come up in this bitch. Look where we live, man. In hell. I think they want somebody to tell them that you not in here so that they won't have to come. Just lay low for a few days."

"You know I can't do that." I sighed. "If I don't leave out of here at least once a day I'll go crazy."

"Well all I can say is don't get caught," he said giving me a pound. He took a deep breath and looked at Fortune who was now dancing. She was rotating her head and her long gold hair was falling over her face, arms and shoulders. You could barely see her eyes.

Trying to get my mind off of Wicked who was still grilling me I said to WB, "I remember when you first got her that wig."

He laughed. "When I get it?"

"You don't remember when she was dancing by The Pit like she is now?" She had the red wig at the time, but it stopped at her ears. She kept shaking her head and shit, but the hair wasn't long enough to cover her face so it kept throwing the show off."

"Oh shit," he yelled, as he laughed into his hand. "That's right. She was blowing the hell out of me that night. Old girl is many things but pretty ain't one of them."

I laughed harder because he was speaking gospel. "All you kept saying, more hair, more hair," I paused, "so that she could put more hair in her face. You don't remember that shit?"

By now the meaty scent of the hot dogs caused my stomach to rumble, and I was tempted to snatch one off the grill half cooked. Mothafuckas from the West started coming outside too, trying to get in good with East Wingers because they could smell the grub. I can't stand them niggas. Always begging but never sharing when they got shit.

"You right, man."

"You said one day I'm going to buy her a new wig."

"And I did too," he responded.

I remembered that day like it was yesterday. It was the first time I realized that although WB was cool, it was easy for niggas to act a little jealous at times too.

We were in front of the Korean store bumming for dollars that day. We only collected five dollars between me, WB, Gage and Spirit up to that point. When these three girls walked to the bus stop, WB put the cup on the ground and tried to act like he wasn't begging. I didn't know what he was doing so I stepped to him about it.

"What you doing, man?" I asked him when I saw him sit the cup down. I didn't even see the chicks at that time.

"What you talking about?" he leaned against the wall and looked over at the girls. "I'm chilling."

"But we need enough money for food tonight," I reminded him. "

"Give me a second, Mad."

When I focused in the direction he was looking, I understood what held his attention. We lived on the streets, but it didn't curve our appetite for pretty faces and pussy. So I let him live, and let him smile at the pretty girl who was looking in our direction. Except instead of the girl smiling at him, she was staring at me. At first I didn't think WB noticed because of the confident way he was acting.

"Hey, cutie, what's your name?" he asked her.

She rolled her eyes and said, "Boy, ain't nobody thinking about your dusty black ass." She looked over at me. "But his fine ass can get the business anytime he want it."

The look in WB's eyes was harsh. It was as if he wanted to kill her if he was closer. I never saw him look so evil before, and at the moment I started to wonder if he was responsible for Rose's murder. Despite her being interested in me, I didn't give the bitch the time because I didn't like how she carried my friend, but it didn't make him feel any better.

"It's funny how bitches think you a dude. I should tell her."

"For what?"

"For trying to play me."

He didn't do it. Instead he waited for the bus to pull up, and when it did he ran up behind her, pushed her on the bus' steps and snatched her wig off. I don't even know how he knew she was wearing one. We laughed on the way back to The Catacombs until he got quiet.

"You think I'm too black?" he asked me.

"Ain't no such thing as too black," I told him. "You know that shit."

"Well why she ain't want me?"

"Girls be that way sometimes, WB," I said. "They never want you when you want them. It's the story of my life."

When we got back to The Catacombs that day he presented the wig as a gift to Fortune. She loved it.

The thing about Fortune is this. She wanted WB from the moment she laid eyes on him. When WB was sick it was Fortune who was there to nurse him back to health. When WB needed or wanted anything, it was Fortune who would sell her pussy to be sure he got it. Most of the men in The Catacombs fucked Fortune, which is another reason WB couldn't take her seriously. However, her heart belonged to him. But there was something I must say. Nobody knew if Fortune was a girl or dude and I heard when she gets fucked its always in the asshole.

We also believed when Fortune was up top she took too many silicone shots to the face and never got right. Without the bangs on her forehead she was ugly. With all that aside, Fortune was one of the nicest people you could ever wish to meet. So when the lights were low and she got to dancing, we would yell, more hair, more hair! And for that moment she was our Beyoncé.

When the meat was cooked and our stomachs were filled, WB let Wicked and Speedstar share a hot dog, although we were like fuck him at first. He ate and left The Pit without even saying thank you.

When we were done eating WB pulled out a bottle of Hennessy and my eyes lit up. Finally I was feeling like myself again. That is until Wicked came back to The Pit with a new face we didn't recognize.

New faces were trouble. We never knew who you were or what you wanted with us. Sometimes a new member was a homeless person who just gave up on life, but most times they were on the run for some violent crime. So we had to give a new member the *Rights of Passage*, where everyone interested would ask the new member questions before we accepted them.

The last person Wicked brought in ended up being a serial rapist and killer, and nobody could respect Wicked's taste in associates. So this was serious.

"Where you from?" WB asked the New Face.

The New Face tugged on his long knotty dreads. "From Arizona."

"Why you here?" Gage asked with her hands on her hips.

"Don't got nowhere else to go I guess," he shrugged.

"Why don't you got a place to go?" Spirit continued.

"It's like this," he sighed, "I had sex with my ex-girlfriend's daughter once. She liked it a lot, but her mother got mad 'cause I didn't want to be with her no more. Her daughter was fucking me back and everything. Anyway she told the authorities and I had to leave. It's about to get cold and I don't like being up top. They kill people like us."

I looked at my crew and knew immediately that this dude was bad news. "How old was she?" I asked. "Your lady's daughter?"

"Twelve."

"Nigga, get the fuck out of here before we break your jaw," I said pointing at the exit.

He looked back at Wicked who was staring at me with hate in his eyes. "Do I really gotta leave, man," he asked. "I thought you said it was cool. You said that everybody here has a past and that they would accept me."

We all waited for Wicked to confirm what we already knew. It ain't up to Wicked. It's up to us. *All of us.* "You gotta go, man, I'll get up with you later," Wicked confirmed.

When New Face left, Wicked rushed up to me and stared me down. I could tell that he wanted to do something to me, but if this dude puts his hands on me I'm going to kill him. Instead of touching me he turned around and looked at everyone.

"Did ya'll know that this bitch wears a plastic dick under her jeans?" he asked everyone.

My heart dropped into the pit of my stomach.

"What you doing, Wicked?" Gage asked. "Why you out here tripping?"

"Ain't nothing going on with me," he rubbed his crouch. "I got what she wants. A dick. She on the other hand running 'round here faking like she a nigga."

"Who cares," the Parable said walking up to us. His voice was strong and when he moved the crowd separated. His skin was really gray and I could never tell if he was black or white. The jeans he was wearing were so worn at the bottom that they raised to his knees. "Who cares what he's holding between his legs? I got a peg leg and Fortune been stuffing her titties with old newspapers for years. You gonna fuck with us too?"

Fortune gasped.

"I got nothing but respect for you, old man," Wicked said to him. "But I'm talking about this bitch right here. You don't have nothing to do with this shit."

"I don't know much about her past, but I know that in the short time she's been here she's been doing a lot for the community. We don't judge people on their past once we accept them, Wicked. You know that."

"You don't understand," Wicked continued. "She's faking like she a nigga when she's not. And she's lying to everybody too. All I want to do is protect the people who live here."

"You need to be easy, Wicked, just because you roll with blacks don't give you a license to use the word nigga so freely," I said to him. "You been taking way too many liberties with that word and your black card has expired. Plus I know people who have been killed for less."

"You gonna wish you never came here. I promise you." Wicked said angrily.

CHAPTER 6
MAD

I needed to get out of The Catacombs for a minute before I fucked Wicked up so I decided to hang out in front of the Korean Liquor store by myself up the block. Most times if I waited long enough I would run into somebody just like me who was willing to share a bottle.

I was leaning on the brick wall of the store with my baseball cap down over my eyes. I'd seen two police officers earlier in the day and didn't want to take the risk of one of them recognizing me. I also pulled my curly hair back into a tight ponytail, so they couldn't see it from the front.

When a girl sporting the tightest pink shirt I'd ever seen in my life walked up to me, wearing jeans just as tight, my joint jumped. I wanted to fuck her.

"What's your name?" she asked me holding her hand on her hip. "You kinda cute."

"Who's asking and why?" I responded.

She giggled but I was dead serious.

"Oh so what you playing hard to get or something? Your name so top secret that you don't want nobody to know?"

"Listen, I'm not looking to make new friends. So either get to the point or step out my face."

"Like you so busy you can't afford to give me a little convo. You do know that you not no better than me right?"

Silence.

She rubbed her right honey brown arm and said, "You got a loosey on you I can borrow?"

"Naw, I don't smoke right now. I looked away."

"Smoke right now?" she giggled. "What that mean?"

"It means that I don't totally diss smoking, and I do whatever I want that makes me feel good at the time. But right now cigarettes ain't it."

I took my attention off of her because although she was pretty, she was also annoying. I was here to share a bottle with someone who had money, not to rap to some bitch that was bumming just like me.

But instead of leaving Pink Shirt stayed next to me, just on the other side of the door of the store. I was kinda blown because if someone with a bottle had it to share, who would they give it to? Me? A girl who looked like a dude who wasn't fucking? Or her? The pretty friendly one in the pink shirt with her nipples poked out.

My worst-case scenario happened when some old man walked up to the store, turned his head right and said, "You sure are a pretty little thing."

Pink Shirt grinned, looked at me and said, "Thank you."

I couldn't make out what he said next but I do know that he walked into the store, and fifteen minutes later he came out and handed her a pack of cigarettes along with a fifty-dollar bill. When they exchanged numbers and he left, she walked over to me.

"You want one?" she asked holding the pack of Kools out in my direction.

I shook my head no and avoided eye contact with her. I was hoping that since she got what she wanted, she would beat it and let me have the store now. It was getting late and that's when all of the good drunks came out.

"You don't talk much do you?"

I shook my head no again. *Damn, kick rocks already!*

"You drinking?" she asked me. She pulled out the fifty dollar bill and it was the prettiest thing I seen in a minute.

Now she had my attention. "What you really asking?"

"Well I was going to buy a bottle. But since I don't have a favorite liquor, I was wondering what you liked. I got the money so don't worry about pitching in." She flashed her yellow teeth. "This one is on me."

"Why you gonna do that?"

She exhaled. "I'm lonely and all I want to do is spend a little time with somebody. I promise I don't want nothing else. Just some convo and a little time. You got it to spare?"

I guess shawty turned out not to be too bad after all.

⬤━━━━━━━━━━━━━━━━━━━━━━━━━⬤

Since we were obviously both homeless, and I knew I couldn't take her back to The Catacombs, we sat on some cardboard boxes in the alley next to the store. She bought a big bottle of Hennessy, and after awhile I realized we had a lot in common. We both came from violent homes and were born to women who preferred the streets over us.

"I don't hate my mother," she said taking a large gulp, "I just don't like how she raised me. It's kind of hard to explain." She handed me the bottle.

"Trust me," I said taking a swig before handing the bottle back to her, "I get you. My mother wasn't the best person in the world either, but I guess you learn to deal with it."

She smiled. "My mother was a heroin addict for fifteen years before she thought she could fly. She was always doing something so I never worried. The crazy part is before she walked up to the top of our apartment building, raised her arms and jumped off I always thought she was invincible. Even when I watched her fall I expected wings to pop from her back." She shook her head. "When her brains decorated the curb I knew that was a lie. And you know what, to this day I expect her to come back to me."

I just nodded. I couldn't relate on that part because I hated my mother when she was alive and I hate her more now that she's dead.

"You wanna fuck?" she asked me out of nowhere.

"Got a place?" I responded drinking the rest of the Henny.

"No," she grinned, "but I know a place."

●━━━━━━━━━━━━━━━━━━━━━━━━●

I was on the floor of a supply closet, in an apartment building, fucking the dog shit out of Choosey. At least that's what I thought her name was because when she told me I was buzzing too hard to hear straight. It wouldn't matter after I got mine anyway so I didn't ask her to repeat it.

Choosey was laying flat on her back with nothing on but her shirt. My jeans were pulled down, and I had one hand on her ankle until I used one of my fingers to flip her clit. As the dildo pressed against my joint and I moved into her body, I felt invincible. Choosey's pussy was dripping wet, and her pink clit stuck out of her body like a button. She smelled a little musty but I didn't give a fuck. Plus if she kept looking at me the way she was doing I was going to bust in a second and it wouldn't matter anyway.

And that's exactly what happened when she bit down on her bottom lip and squeezed her titties so hard they turned red. I felt like I exploded inside of her.

The moment I got mine off, I started looking at her differently. She didn't look like the sexy girl in the pink shirt anymore. She was a whore just like my mother, and I hated her for it. I immediately tried to think of a good excuse to bounce.

Maybe I'll tell her that I have to go to work in the next hour. Or maybe I'll tell her that my friend is going to meet me somewhere in fifteen minutes and that I forgot about it until now.

"That was so good," she said looking in my eyes as I struggled to pull my clothes up. "You fine?"

I didn't respond. Why do I despise her so much right now? She a gutter whore who's fucking niggas outside the liquor store. But since I hit the pussy what does that say about me?

"You okay?" she asked sliding back into her jeans. "You look different now. Like you not having a good time no more. Did I do something wrong? I can lick it if you want. My mother taught me that too before she died."

"What?" I frowned. "Fuck no!"

On the sly I rubbed my dildo on her jeans to wipe off her body juice. Then I reconnected it to the strap.

"Naw, I'm good," I responded and yawned. "Just kind of tired that's all."

I stood up and looked down at her. I decided against making up some fake ass story on why I wanted to leave. I was just going to tell her I was ready to bounce, and that it was nice knowing her.

That was until she said, "Hey, I'm going to get us another bottle of liquor? Feel like hanging out with me a little while longer? I sure could use the company."

She sure did know how to court a nigga.

———————————————●———————————————

Someone was dragging me by my legs and pulling me on the streets of DC. When I looked to my right, I saw people at the bus stops holding conversations as I slid by them. The last thing I remember was Choosey getting more money from three different dudes and us drinking bottle after bottle in the alley. I do know she sucked their dicks for the money and I smelled the funk on her breath when she talked. I guess after that I went into the Drunk Zone.

When stuff started getting darker I finally focused on who was pulling my legs, which caused my back to scratch against the concrete in the process. It was Fierce, and he smiled down at me. Spirit, Gage and WB were beside him and they looked angry. I guess they found me passed out somewhere up the block and were taking me back to the place I dreaded. The Catacombs.

CHAPTER 7
MAD

The subway seemed rockier today as I sat the long way across a seat. My soda bottle was filled with Hennessey and I was thinking about my life. My back still burned from being drug on the street by my ankles by Fierce.

Although I know I live in The Catacombs, the best part about it is not being there. Plus I never know how I'm going to handle myself around Wicked. I feel like I'm five seconds from unleashing on him and if I do where will I end up?

Last night I thought a lot about my mother. It's never good when she comes to my mind because I hate her so much it gives me nightmares. I remember the days she starved my twin sister and me. I remember the days she burned me with an iron until it ran cold. I remember how I watched her fuck a man over the arm of the sofa in the living room, which caused Mr. Nice Guy, the only man who ever loved me to get murdered in my face. I hate that bitch so much that sometimes I can feel it all over my body. As if I'm possessed by her.

When I was not thinking about her, I was thinking about my son. He'll never know that I brought him into this world and that even though I saw him once, I love him more than I could ever show him.

The last time I saw my son was outside Harmony's funeral. I didn't plan on going to the funeral, which is why when I showed up it was already over. To tell you the truth I don't know what made me go. Maybe I wanted to see my twin sister who I hadn't seen in months at that point, or maybe I wanted to see the casket of my mother being led from the funeral home to the grave, to be sure she was dead. All I know was that when it was all said and done, I was outside of that funeral home. But I never expected to see my sister with my son.

You gotta understand a crack head friend of my crack head grandmother stole my baby from me while I was giving birth. So I thought he was lost forever. Whole time though, Jayden was holding my baby acting like he belonged to her. But I can't provide him with a life. I'm living in a tunnel with no place of my own. I'm not fit to be a person let alone a mother.

I took a large sip of liquor when a group of niggas who looked about my age stepped onto the train. They were all about my height— short. The tallest one, who was wearing a blue jean t-shirt, was also the loudest. Behind him were two other dudes and they seemed to be hanging onto everything he had to say.

"I'm letting everybody on this train know right now, if anybody even look at me funny, I'm busting they face back," Blue Jean Shirt said into the train.

I turned my head and looked out of the window. I could see the graffiti walls flying by in bursts of colors, as the train sped down the track. I turned my head not because I was scared of him, but because I don't feel like the drama today. Besides, the last thing I need is to be getting involved when I'm wanted for murder.

Through the glass I could see Blue Jean Shirt approaching a white kid with a baseball cap flipped to the back. Blue Jean Shirt snatched the cap off of his head and threw it to the floor. Then he got up in the kids face and pointed a long finger at his nose. "What the fuck you doing looking at me? Didn't you hear what I just said earlier?"

"I...I'm not looking at you I..."

I took another sip of liquor and pulled my cap down over my eyes. As bored as I was, this scene was too pathetic to watch.

"Look at him stuttering," one of Blue Jean friend's added. "He look like he about to melt, Vince. I say we beat him down right here for his disrespect."

"How many people think I should kick his ass?" Blue Jean shirt asked everybody around him. "Just say the word and I'll do it."

I fucking hated this dude. If you gonna hit him just do it already. He reminded me of Antwan Bolden. He use to come behind me in elementary school when I lived in Texas, and smack me in the back of the head with this big encyclopedia. He did it every day, until I showed him I wasn't scared of him anymore and hit myself repeatedly in the forehead. I opened an old scar I had on my head at the time and blood poured everywhere on my face. He knew that if I could hurt myself, nobody else could hurt me.

Yeah, this mothafucka was definitely bringing up bad memories.

"Can you please leave my son alone," the white woman asked Blue Jean Shirt. "He didn't mean to stare at you." She was so scared her teeth rattled. "He was just nervous that's all."

"He might not have meant to but he did it anyway right?" he responded. "If you ask me he got a problem with his eyes that I might have to fix."

"Is there anything I can give you to leave us be?" the woman pleaded. "Money or anything?" She raised her purse and he snatched it. "You can have whatever's inside. Just please leave us alone."

Lady, what are you doing? I thought. *He didn't even ask for money.*

Blue Jean Shirt went through the purse and I don't know what happened, but suddenly I was standing behind him. The two dudes who were with him moved out of the way, leaving him exposed. He turned around and looked directly into my eyes. I could smell fear all over him. I don't have any weapons and I have no idea what I'm about to do next but why does he look at me as if I'm the devil?

He said, "What the fuck do you—"

Before he could finish, I gripped his shirt and slammed his face into the glass window of the subway. I did it once, twice, and then so many times until I lost count. He dropped her purse on the seat and he seemed confused. Why am I doing this shit? It's none of my business.

When I was done his blood was splashed all over the window, seat and floor.

Instead of stopping I thought about my drunk mother again. I thought about my evil sister. I thought about not having my son. I thought about living underground, in the worst conditions you could ever imagine. I thought about missing my friends, the original Mad Max and I wondered if they thought about me too. I thought about every painful thing I could and when I stopped he was unconscious.

When I released him, I realized that his friends were on the far end of the train now. I guess they are scared of me too and wanted to move further away.

When I focused back on the lady, who's son was just being bullied, she was holding her son tightly. Instead of being scared of Blue Jean Shirt, they now seemed scared of me. When the train slowed down, and I saw two cops on the outside, I knew I had to bounce.

I raised my bloody hands to show both of them that I meant no harm. "I'm sorry"— I backed up toward the door— "I really am so sorry." When the train stopped I rushed out.

I was lying in Gage's cubby on my bed. I was thinking about the day and how I reacted on the subway. I snap like that all of the time, and I never know when it's coming. Sometimes I scare myself more than I do anybody else. It could've been bad if the cops were paying me any attention. I don't want to go to jail.

My thoughts were stopped when I felt Gage ease into my bed. She had a bed in here too so why she in mine?

She rubbed my arm and I said, "Gage, can you get out of my bed please?"

Her hand felt as if it stiffened. "Mad, I need this. Please." Her voice was hard, and I could hear the pain.

"I can't, Gage. We friends." I told her while I faced the grungy cardboard wall in front of me. I couldn't look at her. "I had a friend like this before and—"

I can't remember the last time I got slapped in the face, but I'll remember this time for as long as I live. Gage came down on my mouth so hard with her hand, that my lips felt flat on my face. After hitting me she hopped out of bed and rushed out of the cubby. Gage cries easily, so I could already hear her.

When she was gone, I turned around and sat up in bed. And when I did I saw Pickles walk into my room. Pickles was the youngest resident of The Catacombs. I don't know who he belonged to but lately he took to me like we shared the same blood.

He's about five years old, and he never had any shoes on. He's a cute little kid, and I think he might be mixed because he got a head full of wild curly hair. Since we don't know who he belonged too, we all took care of him and gave him food.

"What you doing in here, Pickles?" I asked looking over at him. "Why you in my cubby?"

"I'm scared," he said hopping up and down on Gage's bed. "Its too many bugs down there."

"Who you staying with tonight?"

"Uncle Spirit," he said jumping higher. "But he put me out so they can put needles in they arms. But it don't look like it hurt. Why they do that?"

Although I like my drink, I never got off on heroin or crack. If you want to pass a Jay, you can count me in, but anything else I'm not with.

"Uncle Spirit is a grown ass man so you don't need to worry about all that. Did you eat tonight?"

He nodded his head up and down. "Yes, Uncle WB brought me some chips and a soda. I wanted some more but he didn't have any money, and now my tummy growling."

"I'll see if I can get you some tomorrow okay?"

While I watched him hop around the room, just like I thought, Wicked busted inside of the cubby.

"Fuck you do to Gage huh? Why she out there crying?"

I stood up so that he couldn't catch me slipping. "Wicked, you better get out my face. What goes on between me and Gage ain't none of your business. As a matter of fact ain't shit I do none of your business."

"If I don't get out of your face what you gonna do, bitch?" he smirked. "Give me some of that pussy? Because I'm sure it's tight as shit now since nobody fucked it."

I moved to hit him when Spirit pulled him out of the cubby by snatching his arm, and yanking him backwards. "What the fuck is going on?" Spirit asked both of us. "Why ya'll in here fighting? It's one o'clock in the morning."

"This nigga got Gage crying, Spirit," Wicked told him. "I keep telling ya'll mothafuckas not to trust her. But nobody listening to me. I think she hit her or something the way she was acting."

"I know Gage didn't run to you and tell you that shit, Wicked," Spirit said. "I just saw her a minute ago. So what you doing down here in the East anyway? At this time of night? Snooping?"

"I was…I was…" I guess he couldn't think of a good lie because he stopped talking.

"Wicked, we agreed that you wouldn't come down here unless you leaving the tunnel. And we wouldn't come down there unless we let somebody know. So just bounce, okay?"

Wicked looked as if he wanted to hit me until Pickles threw a rock at his head. Wicked moved toward him like he was going to hit him and I blocked his path. "Get the fuck out my room," I told Wicked. I pointed at the exit. "Bounce."

Wicked looked at Pickles once more and said, "Yeah aight."

When he left I sat on the bed and Pickles sat next to me. When he put his feet over my legs, I knew immediately why they called him Pickles. His feet smelled like a large bottle of white vinegar.

"You gonna be good, man?" Spirit asked. "I know you wanted to kill him when he came in here but I'm glad you kept your cool."

"Yeah, I'll be fine. Fuck that nigga. Anyway, what you doing down here?"

"I was coming to tell you that we found another body in The Catacombs. They don't know who it is or where it came from. But you already know what I think."

"Yeah, that Wicked had something to do with it," I said. "Just like I think he had something to do with Rose." When I realized I was preaching to the choir I said, "Anyway, where Gage?"

"She's in my cubby. She's not coming back tonight so don't expect her."

"Can you tell her I'm sorry? I didn't mean to go at her like that. It's just that, I mean, I'm not feeling her in that way."

"Can I ask you something?"

"Shoot."

"Why don't you look at her like that?" he asked me.

"I don't have a lot of reasons outside of us being cool. I think she took some of the things I did for her as a friend and assumed that it was more than what it was."

"Do you think she'll ever look at me like that? Like somebody she'd want to be with?""

"I think you should come out and tell her how you feel. Other then that, man, I can't call it. I mean, you a cool dude and all and I don't see why not."

He doesn't seem convinced. "Okay, well, I'll get up with you later okay?"

I gave him some dap and he walked out, leaving Pickles and me alone. When I saw Pickles looking down at something, I asked him what he had in his hand.

"A book," he said holding it up. "I'm going to read you a bedtime story, okay?"

I grinned. "What you know about bedtime stories?"

"Nothing," he shrugged. "But lay down and close your eyes."

Although I knew he couldn't read, I laid down anyway. He sat Indian style right next to my pillow and the stank of his skin burned my nose. I made mental notes to get him cleaned up tomorrow. Outside of my crew, not many people cared much about hygiene down here. And even they thought I went overboard because I wiped dirt off of my shoes every hour and kept fresh boxers.

"Once upon a time a mean old lady left the baby by himself and never came to see him again…"

I drifted off to sleep while listening to the story that resembled my life.

CHAPTER 8
MAD

I sat in Gage's cubby squeezing my legs tightly together. I don't know what's going on but earlier today I went to the restroom to pee and it hurt so bad I screamed. I hope that bitch I fucked didn't burn me. A lot of people at The Catacombs had contracted everything from crabs to HIV and I didn't want to be like them.

"Mad, watch this shit," Fish said to me.

He was on the outside of the cubby and I was on the inside but from where I was I could still see him. When I finally saw what he was doing I felt like punching him in the back of the head. This dude had a sling shot and he was putting rats into it. Then he flung them against the wall.

"Aye, Fish, take that shit down to the West, man," I pointed to the right, "I ain't trying to see that shit right now. I don't feel good."

"Why?" he asked with wide eyes. "They all over the place. This way we can get rid of some of them and have fun too. You wanna try it?"

"The shit gross, man. I'm not trying to see you slam no nasty ass rats against the wall. Fuck is wrong with you anyway? Get from in front of my cubby with that bullshit. I'm not going to tell you again."

He exhaled. "But we ain't got nothing else to do around here, plus these mothafuckas are everywhere. I figure we might as well make a sport out of it."

"Man, take it down west before I get up and go the fuck off." It's bad enough I'm in pain and he outside of my cubby doing dumb shit.

You know what this nigga does? He scoops the dead rats up and stomps toward the West Wing. I just shook my head and laid back on my bed. I don't understand what the fuck is going on with my body. I don't have health insurance so what was I going to do?

I'm about to lose my mind when all of the lights go out in The Catacombs. Without light you're submerged into pitch-blackness. And the longer the lights are out the quicker the rats and bugs would take over.

"Remain calm, remain calm," E1 yelled into the tunnel. I didn't know where he was but I could hear his voice clearly. "I got this under control and we'll have the lights back on in no time."

It wasn't until I saw him walk past the front of my cubby with a flashlight that I knew where he was. I walked behind him and his son who was carrying a ladder, wondering what they were about to do to get the lights back on.

"What's wrong, E1?" I asked following them. "Why the power go out?"

"They probably cut us off upstairs," he said as he stomped hurriedly toward the crossroads. "Whenever the lights go off like that, the electric company detected a surge not accounted for and they do a reset we lose electricity. It's not a problem though, I got it."

I don't know why, but for some reason I feel like something bad is about to happen. Maybe it's this pain I have rushing between my legs that I'm sure is some funky STD. Or maybe it's the darkness that secretly creeps me out.

When we made it to the middle of the crossroads E2 set up the ladder so that E1 could climb to the top of the light pole. He shined the flashlight up so that his father could see what he was doing. When I turned around into the darkness of the tunnel I saw Spirit and Gage moving toward me with a flashlight.

"Mad, you okay," Spirit asked. "I didn't see you in the cubby so I'm glad you down here. Fish said you were in pain."

"Yeah, man, I'm good. Just gotta see if Old Man Young got something for me." I looked at Gage again. She was still mad at me for not fucking her.

Instead of giving her any attention, I focused on E1 on the ladder. I wanted to learn how he did what he did. He was up there for a few minutes before power was restored.

When I turned around to look at Spirit and Gage again, I heard Gage scream. "Oh my, God, Everest! I can't believe you're back! You're finally back!"

I knew something bad was going to happen. And there she was.

●————————————————————————————————●

We were all in Spirit's room and this Everest chick wouldn't stop talking. Her long black braids hung over her right shoulder and she reminded me a little of my ex-girlfriend Glitter. The only difference is that I hate this Everest bitch.

Everest told Gage, Spirit, WB and Fierce about all of her fake ass adventures, and they hung onto everything she said as if it were true. What made me even madder was that she kept looking over at me every time she said something.

When she told them how she went to the top of the Eifel tower, I noticed that Spirit seemed out of the conversation. Maybe he didn't believe her either. So I walked over to him and said, "You wanna talk, man?"

He stood up and left the cubby without answering me. I took it as a cue to go with him into the hallway. Even then I could feel Everest's eyes on me. Why is she always watching me?

We stood by the doorway, but out of earshot of everyone inside. In a low voice I asked, "What's up, Spirit? You not feeling good either?"

I was thinking of my own pain too.

"What's wrong with me Old Man Young can't fix. So I'll be fine."

"So you gonna lie to me? Everybody knows you the most levelheaded person out of all of us, so I can tell something's wrong. You not alright."

He sighed. "It's my sister."

Although I knew Spirit did something to avenge his sister, because he was on the run too, I never knew what because he would never talk about it. "What about her?"

"She died in a fire five years ago," he looked down at his feet. "It was because of an arsonist...some dude she fucked with back in the day. I don't like talking about it because it makes me want to start doing things I shouldn't." He looked into my eyes and I saw murder. "You know?"

My heart thumped. "I'm sorry, man. I experienced loss but I didn't lose a sister to death. Is there anything I can do?"

He shook his head. "Naw, I got a bump back in my cubby. I'm going to shoot up when everybody leaves. Want some?"

"You know I don't fuck around." I paused. "How did your sister die?" I asked. "I know it was a fire but how did it start?"

"Come on, Mad, you know we don't ask questions about the past life unless somebody volunteers information."

"I know, man," I said looking down at my fingers. "I just figured that since you bringing it up, that you'd—"

Spirit interrupted me by waving at Fish who passed us on his way to the exit of The Catacombs. When he was gone Spirit took a deep breath, looked down at the ground and back into my eyes. "I never told anybody this before."

"And you don't have to now if you don't want to, man. I just extended the invite so you could get it off your chest."

"My sister's name was Hui Chen, and she was my twin."

Wow, I never knew he had a *twin* sister before now. We had more in common than I realized.

"She was an artist, and loved painting murals on the sides of buildings around New York. She was pretty good too, and one day someone recognized her work and wanted her to do something for a movie project. I think it was a documentary on street based artists." He sighed. "Well, she met this man and he was way older than her. He was the director in charge of the project and he fell for her. They fell for each other I think.

"My sister was 17 at the time and he was 40. I was upset because I thought he was taking advantage of her since he was younger. Before I knew it my sister got pregnant and he tried to force her to get an abortion. Turns out he was married, and didn't want his wife finding out about her. But my sister refused, because it goes against our beliefs. She broke up with him and moved. He couldn't leave her alone and he eventually caught up with her, tied her to the passenger seat of her car, drove her to a secluded area and set the car on fire."

"Damn…"

"It made me not care about life anymore after that shit, Mad," he said softly. "She was such a great person, and she didn't deserve to go out like that. Anyway the trial went to court and he got out after a year. The dude had a history as an arsonist and he'd killed hundreds, but they could never catch him before he killed my sister. He never answered to his crime. I'm talking about the fact that he didn't do one day in prison, Mad. His lawyer got him off on some technicality and he walked. My parents were guilt ridden after that shit and died from broken hearts. It made me feel worthless. So after I helped bury my parents I caught up with him on the set of one of his movies and I stabbed him to death. Right in front of everybody. At first people thought it was a prank, or relating to the movie but when he didn't move and I pulled the bloody knife out of his chest they knew it was serious. So I went on the run after that." He finally looked at me. "And before I knew it I ended up here." He looked up into the ceiling. "In this tomb."

I didn't know what to say.

"What made you tell me your story?"

"The rest of the gang loves me, but I don't think they really want to know what I've been through. I feel like you were really strong enough to take some of the load for me. So I told you."

"Thanks, I think." I paused. "I just want to—"

"Is everything okay?" Everest asked walking up behind us.

Something about her voice made me pause. I can't like this bitch. I won't like this bitch.

"Everything cool," Spirit said kissing her on the cheek. "I'm going back inside now." He walked off.

I was about to follow him until she extended her hand in front of me.

"Hi, I'm Everest. And you are?"

"Not interested," I said walking around her and back to Spirit's place. "And stay the fuck away from me."

CHAPTER 9

MAD

"You have a urinary tract infection, you're not burning," Old Man Young said to me as I stood in the entrance of his cubby. "I tasted your urine and it was sweet. You'll be okay."

What the fuck?

"How do you know that from drinking my piss?" I asked observing the surroundings. "And why the fuck are you drinking it?" I frowned.

He had so many books in his spot that I didn't know where he slept. And half of the books in his room are half eaten by rats. But he picked up a dark blue hardcover book with gold writing and approached me. "Outside of tasting the sweetness of your urine, you said it hurts when you piss correct?" He looked inside of the book, and ran his finger slowly from left to right over the words.

"Yes," I nodded.

"And you say you have pain on one side of your back correct?"

I rubbed my lower back, although I'm not sure why. "Yes. It hurts like shit too."

"Well you have a urinary tract infection." He slammed the book closed and tossed it on the floor. It landed next to the rest of his chewed up books. "It's as simple as that, so you can relax some. You'll be okay."

"Relaxing is the last thing I feel like doing right now. This shit is killing me."

He turned around and walked deeper into his cubby-hole. He flung shirt after shirt on the floor until he found a red one. With the red shirt in his hand he dug into the pocket and pulled out a pill bottle. He approached me and handed me the bottle.

"That will help. Take one everyday with food."

I looked at the bottle. "What is it?"

"The cure. As long as you don't miss a day, you'll be good. I got them from a pharmacy awhile back from one of the residents."

I frowned. "But how did I get this shit?"

"Do you drink lots of liquid?"

"Of course," I said thinking about the Hennessey I downed before even coming to see him. "I drink something everyday." I smiled. "At least I try."

He lowered his head. "I'm talking about water, Mad."

"Water?" I frowned shaking my head. "Naw, what I want with water outside of washing up in it?"

"Listen, I love liquor like the next man. In fact I drink it everyday just like you. But my love for the bottle is also the reason I have cirrhosis of the liver, am severely under-weight, and I have jaundice which give me these yellow eyes"— he widened them— "I also bruise easily and I'm always tired too. Now I'm not going to tell you how to live your life. After all"— he looked up into the grungy tunnel's ceiling— "who am I to give advice considering my lifestyle? But I will say this, if you want to be like me you keep on drinking how you're drinking and you will. I figure I got about six more months in me before I keel over. I wonder how much time you got?"

I don't say anything. I heard what he said but I do know this, I'm not gonna stop drinking no time soon. I'll just add some water to my routine until I get rid of this situation.

"Thanks for the pills," I said tugging on my cap. "I'll get up with you later."

"Thank you my ass. That medicine gonna run you a bottle of vodka."

As I walked down the east wing leading to the crossroads, I was holding a bucket of water in one hand, and Pickle's hand in the other. Inside of the bucket was a bar of soap, and two new washcloths hung on the rim. I also cut open a box and stuffed it under my arm.

Once I made it to The Crossroads, I banged a left to walk toward the shower area, the place where most people wash up. I put the flashlight on the ledge. "Aight, Pickles, I'm gonna wash you up okay?"

He looked up at me like I was speaking Chinese.

"What's wash up?"

Damn. Little Yo ain't been clean in forever. He don't even know what it means.

"It's when I clean your body and your feet so that they won't funk up me and Gage's cubby. Get it now?" He giggled. "So that's funny huh? That you be out here stinking and shit?" I joked.

"Yes," he smiled again.

I shook my head and took the bar of soap out of the bucket. I also took off his shorts and dirty shirt. I'm going to have to get him some gear because he's been wearing this outfit forever.

When I removed his clothes I noticed that he had all kinds of rat bites over his body. I tried to act like it wasn't nothing but I'm fucked up by seeing the condition of his skin.

After I washed Pickles, I put back on his dirty clothes. Since there was still some clean water left, I stepped a little away, pulled my pants down a little and washed myself up with the other rag. Normally I wouldn't do it here, but the restaurant I usually go to was closed for renovations. As I freshened up he stood on the cardboard box and when I saw he was watching me, I stepped further away from him and wiped my joint, but when I wiped the washcloth across the place where my breasts use to be. The bruise on my body was a constant reminder of my past.

A few years ago my sister's ex-boyfriend raped me. The day he violated me stayed with me always. After the rape I was placed in a hospital where my father came in and gave me a scalpel. He knew how much I hated my female body so he told me if I wanted to have my breasts removed, that I should dig into them there. Since I was at a hospital it was the best place because at least they had to save me. In my breasts' place was a mutilated chest and I like it better that way.

I'm almost finished when I heard a loud scream. Something was always happening here. I poured the water out and threw everything in the bucket. Pickles grabbed it and we both headed in the direction of the screams, which was toward the East Wing. The drama was right in front of Spirit's cubby. The rest of Mad MaXXX was looking at Fish and some woman.

"What's going on?" I asked Spirit. Pickles stood next to me.

"That's Fish's mother," he whispered. "She found out he lived here and came in to get him. They said she didn't even use a flashlight. Just kept walking until she found him."

"Wait, she came into the Tunnel without light?" I never heard of anything like that before.

"Yep! It fucked me up too, Mad. I guess she really love the nigga."

I looked at her again. She didn't look like a superhero. In my opinion she was average, but there had to be strength in her because walking inside is not for the weak at heart. "Did she come in by herself?"

"Yep!"

As I watched her try to pull Fish out of the tunnel a feeling came over me. And I knew it was wrong which was why I tried to push it away. If he had a mother who cared about him I wondered why he was down here with us. My mother never gave a fuck about what I did just as long as I was home when the social worker came so she could get her check. I had no idea where my father was, and I'm sure he forgot about me too. Even if he did care he wouldn't come here.

"Fish, I love you," his mother said grabbing his hand. "And I don't know what you're doing here with these people but I want you home. I don't care about you being on drugs anymore. We can get you help, son. Just please come home with me. Your family misses you so much and I miss you too."

"You think he'll leave with her?" someone asked me.

When I turned around I was staring into Everest's pretty face. I hate that I think she's cute because I want her to go away. But since the first day she got here she always seemed to be following me, and I never knew why.

"I don't know if he'll leave with her or not," I said with an attitude. "It ain't my business like it ain't yours."

I turned around and walked toward Gage's cubby. I could tell by the soft thud of Everest's tennis shoes that she was following me.

I stopped and turn around. "Look, I don't like you," I told her. "So stay the fuck away from me aight?"

"You've been hurt before haven't you?" she asked me.

"Shawty, you don't even know the half."

CHAPTER 10
MAD

I walked quickly down the DC sidewalk, feeling like I could commit murder again if I wanted to. I was so sure of it that I stared into the face of everybody who I passed on the street. I wanted one person, just one, to give me a reason to unleash. I'm sick of the bullshit that goes on in The Catacombs, and I'm even madder for not having any place else to go to get away from it. I need a getaway for real. Maybe Fish's mother made me feel bad for not having anybody in my life.

I thought I got my wish for a release when a pretty light skin chick with long black hair pulled up on the side of me. She was driving a black BMW, and she looked good pushing it too.

She rolled down the passenger window and asked, "You need a ride?"

I was immediately suspicious. Why would a chick looking like her pull up on somebody who looked like me? I was about to step off until I realized that since she was driving the BMW, she had way more at risk than I did. I might as well take a chance. Besides, what else did I have to lose?

"Yeah, you gonna give me one?" I responded tugging my cap.

The lock to the passenger door popped up and she said, "Get in, cutie."

I climbed into the car and looked her over while she drove. She was wearing a red Gucci tank top and some black jeans. The car smelled like new and it was sparkling clean. I even peeped the red on the bottoms on her shoes and the brown Louis Vuitton purse that was open in the backseat with a few hundred-dollar bills stuffed inside.

For a moment I pretended like this was my car and she was my bitch. When I realized I would never be rich I felt dumb.

"What's your thing?" I asked. "For real. Women like you don't approach niggas like me."

She smiled. "My thing is whatever you want it to be." She continued to drive and I continued to watch her some more. She seemed confident. When she pulled up on a liquor store she parked. "You drink?"

"Yeah," I said still giving her the one eye. "But I don't have no money."

"I didn't ask you that. All I want to know is what's your poison?"

I sat back into her cream leather seat. "Grab a fifth of Hennessy."

When I gave her my order she acted like it was nothing. She snatched a one hundred dollar bill out of her purse and hopped out of the car. I had to blink three times to be sure I wasn't seeing things. Shawty left the keys to her BMW in the ignition and her Louis V purse in the backseat. I could've pulled this car off or at the very least took the purse and ran, but I was even more interested. She was testing me and I decided to play along.

Ten minutes later she returned with two bottles of Hennessey and some chips. "I grabbed them in case you wanted something to munch on. We can stop to get something to eat later if you're still hungry."

She pulled off and I popped open the Doritos bag. I leaned the bag toward her to see if she wanted any but she shook her head no. "I gotta know what's up with you? This is too good to be true. Where I'm from a day like this is like hitting the lotto."

"You looking too much into this," she grinned. "Just trust me and have fun, because that's all I want from you."

"Then why you picking up strange people walking off the street?"

"You strange?" she asked. "You seem pretty ordinary to me."

"In all of your life you've never met a nigga like me."

"Listen, all I want to know is if I can make you famous?" she paused as she focused on the road ahead of her. "Can I?" she looked at me briefly.

I thought about what I was doing today. Nothing.

"You can make me anything you want."

We were in a nice hotel and I just finished taking a shower and putting on some fresh clothes that she picked up for me in the hotel lobby downstairs. I was lying in the bed, with a bunch of pillows behind my head feeling like I was in heaven. The chick that I now knew as Farah Cotton, because I saw her driver's license when she went into the shower, was standing at the foot of the bed with a sly smile on her face. She was wearing a red bra and matching panties. She was bad.

"You look like you're buzzing over there," she said to me. "I like that. Drunk sex is always the best." She crawled on top of me, straddled me and I removed her bra. "And you clean up real good too."

"Thanks, sexy," I said trying to maintain my cool when all I wanted to do was fuck the shit out of her. Hard too.

"You ready to have a good time? I know I am."

"I been ready," I winked.

She kissed me on the side of my face and then the other cheek. She was about to lift up my shirt until I grabbed her wrist.

"I get it," she smiled. "You one of them girl types who don't like to be touched. You won't have no more problem with me though. Like I said all I want is to have a good time. So let me. Okay?"

Silence.

She bent down and kissed me. She stuffed a lot of tongue into my mouth and I could feel her warm pussy through the shorts I was wearing. She used the same toothpaste I used in the bathroom, so her kiss was minty.

"You know how to kiss," she said looking into my eyes. Our faces were so close now that she looked cross-eyed. It was kind of blowing my mood. "I like that."

I kissed her again and tilted my head.

"You don't talk much do you?" she asked me.

I shook my head no.

"The mysterious type, huh?"

I shrugged.

"You got family out here?" she ran her finger over my chin. "Anybody who may come looking for you if you stay out to late with me?"

"Naw, I'm out here by myself. Time's not a factor in my life."

"I'm going to cut the lights out okay?"

She hopped off of me and it took my eyes a second to adjust to the darkness. Although I couldn't see her clearly after blinking twice, I could see her silhouette. She bent down and kissed me on the neck and for some reason I liked it. Her tongue ran back and forth slowly.

Things were warming up until she removed her mouth and I felt a sharp pain next to my jugular vein. I was about to scream but then she followed it up by sucking on my neck hard. Not knowing what the fuck was going on, I pushed her off and ran over to the wall to turn the light on. When I did I couldn't believe what I saw. Her mouth was covered in my blood and I put my hand on my neck. It was bleeding. Next to her was a silver razor blade that was shiny red.

"What the fuck is you doing?" I yelled. "Why you cut me?"

She looked deranged dripping in my blood. "Come on, baby, I'm just having fun. Aren't you into pain and pleasure?" She got up and moved toward me like a lion.

I can't remember being more scared in my life.

"If you take another step I'm going to kill you," I said grabbing my pants off of the floor and sliding into them. "Do you hear me?"

She stopped in place. "With what? The plastic dick you have strapped between your legs?" She frowned.

This bitch was a lunatic so I turned the knob on the door trying to get out but she slammed it shut. We were wrestling against the door and I was doing all I could to get away from her. But the liquor felt like it was weighing me down and I couldn't fight back the way I use to. I think she may have drugged me. Before I knew it she had me pinned to the floor with a firm finger against my lips.

"Shhh," she said looking down at me. "You might as well give into this, baby. Think about it for a moment, you are a bum. You are homeless and you have nowhere to go. You might as well sacrifice yourself over to me and be famous for it. You wouldn't believe who you are in the presence of now."

My body shivered and I tried to be calm. I could be wrong but something told me she got off on seeing my fear. If I got out of this again I would never fuck with somebody off the street again.

"And who the fuck are you?"

"They call me the DC Vampire because I love to taste a little blood from time to time. But unlike the shit you see in fairy tale books, I don't have any special powers. I'm just a woman who loves inflicting pain and you will be my latest victim."

She was about to bend down and suck on me again until I slammed my fist into the side of her face. She was caught off guard and held onto her eye while I pushed her off of me and was able to get out of the door.

I was half way down the block, and outside of the hotel before I looked back to see if she was chasing me. I decided that I was done with drinking.

*Well…*for now anyway.

CHAPTER 11
MAD

It's *Tell All Tuesday* in The Catacombs. We are standing around The Pit and the fire was going high. Although we normally don't talk about our past lives outside of the tunnel this was the one time a person could speak about their past if they chose. The rule was that anything shared could not be brought up later. Truthfully I was willing to talk about anything accept the cut on my neck everybody kept asking me about. I had nightmares for days behind that crazy bitch.

As I listened to Speedstar talk about her life, I could see the pain on her face. We know she fucked Wicked but after they had sex he dissed her whenever she tried to come around him. She would cry all hours of the night and I would have to tell Gage to turn the music on just so I could get some sleep. Wicked didn't care about what she felt, or how he treated her. And he told her several times to her face, in public. The only reason he had sex with her was to get back at Gage, but I don't think it ever worked. Gage was done and she spent most of her time trying to convince me that she could do me right, when all I wanted to do was be left alone.

Even though I thought what Speedstar did to Gage was wrong I felt connected to Speedstar's story about her mother. Up until this point I never thought it was possible that anyone had a mother worse than mine. I guess I was wrong.

"…My mother would come home early from work sometimes," she said as she stared into the fire like it was showing her the past all over again. "She was evil, and I never knew what sparked her early days home. Maybe they were just to mess with my mind you know?" She looked up at us, and the orange glow from the fire made her eyes sparkle. "That day I wasn't comfortable at home even though she wasn't normally there that early. I had a feeling she would pop up. One of the worst times I remember was during a winter storm. She came home early, only to make me get undressed before pushing me outside of the house. She was high and drunk as usual. For no reason." She wiped the tears from her eyes.

"After awhile being out there with no clothes and shoes on the snow made my feet feel as if they were being poked by tiny needles. I wanted to come inside so badly but my mother just looked at me standing there naked. She was smiling. I saw her running her hands over her breasts. And I knew she was fingering herself as I begged her to come inside. It wasn't until I heard her moan loudly that she let me come back in. She was a sadist but I didn't find out until later. All I wanted her to do was love me, and to be a mother, but she never could. Why couldn't she love me?" she asked looking directly at me.

I couldn't give her an answer. I didn't even know why I couldn't make my mother love me.

Gage went over to hug her, even though she knew she fucked her ex-boyfriend Wicked. Gage put her arm around her and she cried. That shit was powerful. Speedstar's tears fell into the fire. At one point I felt like I should be doing something more, but I didn't know what.

When Speedstar was done sobbing, Gage walked over to me. "Pretty fucked up right?" she asked me.

"Yeah."

"Can I talk to you for a minute?"

I looked away from her, and when I did my eyes rested on Everest. She was staring at me like she always was. What was she thinking?

"What about?"

"I feel like you and I have separated lately, and I want to make that right. It makes me feel bad because I miss you, and you're a good friend."

"I want that too, Gage," I responded looking at her. "I don't want you to have any hard feelings toward me, because it didn't work out." I looked over at Everest again.

"You know she doesn't like you right?" she said with an attitude. Her split personality showed up as usual. "Everybody is attracted to Everest and she never wants anybody. Don't waste your time because she's just a tease. But I'm not."

I felt a lump form in my throat. "I'm not even thinking about that bitch like that. Ya'll be on her dick not me." When I looked up at Gage this time she was gone.

"You don't have to get angry, Mad. I'm just talking."

"And I'm responding. I'm not interested in that girl. What else you want me to say?"

"And you not interested in me either huh?"

Luckily I didn't have to respond when Fierce and Daze from the West Wing came yelling outside into The Pit area. Fierce was quiet and reserved so he never rose his voice unless he was really mad. I knew immediately something was wrong.

"I'm not fucking with you, Daze," Fierce said to him. "Give me back my dope cause I know you took it. You were hanging around the East Wing earlier and everything."

Killer, Daze's girlfriend, was right behind him.

Daze rushed up to Fierce. "You don't know what the fuck you talking about. I didn't take shit from you. I wasn't even in your area. You better get up out of my face."

"You're a fucking lie! I saw you!"

Fierce whipped out a knife and waved it in Daze's direction. He almost caught Killer in the stomach instead since she was close, until I pushed her away. "Don't do this shit, man," I said to Fierce. "Put the knife down before you do something you can't take back."

"You don't understand, Mad, he took my shit from me. I needed that hit. Everybody here takes stuff from me, like I'm some fucking punk! I'm tired of being pushed around out here. I want my respect."

"Then do whatever you gotta do later, Fierce." I looked around, and then lowered my voice so that only he could hear me. "Just not in front of everybody. Your situation is just like mine. You don't have nowhere else to go. Think about this shit."

Fierce observed everybody around The Pit. "I got to be by myself. Before I hurt somebody." He ran out.

●━━━━━━━━━━━━━━━━━━━━━━━━━━━━━━━●

I was in bed the next morning thinking about Speedstar. Before Fierce came to The Pit fighting with Daze I was going to talk to her in private, and tell her I felt her pain. For the first time I was going to go into detail about my life about my abusive mother. It wasn't like we had that type of relationship. I kinda didn't fuck with her because of her connection with Wicked, but I still wanted her to know she wasn't alone.

Even though I was hungry I was about to get up and go look for her before I ate when Spirit walked in. "Hey, did you hear?"

"Hear what?" I sat up in the bed and put my socks on.

"Speedstar left, man. They said down West her cubby is cleaned out and everything."

My heart thumped around a little. "Why she do that?"

"That's what happens sometimes when people *Turn Tell All*. They don't like the way people look at them after knowing their business, so they just leave." He shrugged. "Who knows?" He seemed too nonchalant and I was irritated. "Anyway you coming with us to the soup kitchen? We heard they making baked chicken and rice today. We walking together because we heard they fucking with homeless people again up top too."

"Aight, give me a second though," I told him, not really having an appetite anymore.

When he left I thought about Speedstar. I think I wanted the release for myself more than I did for her. But I guess its better not to share my life with people anyway.

Damn.

CHAPTER 12
MAD

"Help, help, help," Spirit yelled inside of the tunnel.

I heard his voice when I was lying down in the cubby but I thought I was tripping. I never heard him sound so distressed before. I hopped out of bed, and my feet slapped against the flip-flops. Pickles was next to me sleep, so I just pulled the sheets up to his neck so that he could stay in bed. I don't know how it happened, but lately I was left in charge of him. It's a mistake because I can't even take care of myself.

When I looked over where Gage slept, I didn't see her.

When I was outside of my cubby I rushed toward Spirit's voice. When I got to him he was at the entrance of the tunnel, and he was helping Old Man Young inside by his arms. WB was holding the flashlight for us so that we could see where we were going.

"What the fuck happened?" I asked as I grabbed a hold of Old Man Young's legs. He was covered in blood and his eyes were swollen shut.

"They fucking beat him," Spirit said with anger all through his voice. "They caught him slipping and beat him. I don't know if he gonna make it."

We made it to Old Man Young's cubby. "What…why? "I was confused. We sat him on his bed and I looked down at him. There was so much blood I almost didn't recognize him. His left eye was hanging out and he was moaning.

Old Man Young didn't bother anybody. He gave advice to everybody who wanted it and was peaceful. This shit had me wanting to kill.

"Don't you get it yet, Mad," Spirit yelled at me. "They beat him because they could. Because they don't give a fuck about us and they use us as punching bags to take out their problems. That's why they did it."

I'm breathing heavily. I gotta calm down. "Where was he?"

"Out in front of the Korean store. He was sharing a bottle with some dude, when they said that some niggas about our age walked up to them. Dude with Old Man Young was able to get away, but Old Man Young wasn't fast enough. They stomped the fuck out of him, Mad and I don't think he's going to make it." Spirit paced the floor. I could tell his feelings were hurt and I wasn't feeling my best either.

People better be careful around me today. Real careful.

———————————————●———————————————

I'm sitting at the table in the soup kitchen for the second time this week with Spirit, Gage, Fierce, Everest and Pickles. The atmosphere was quiet and I know we all thinking about the same thing. Old Man Young. Earlier we propped him in front of a hospital and ran. His eye rolled out on the ground and everything. Whatever The Parable was doing wasn't working so he needed the professionals. The Parable said he was in a coma the last he heard. But I know he's dead, and it was just a matter of time before we got the news.

"You okay, Mad?" Spirit asked as he sat across from me at the table.

I frowned, and bit my bottom lip. He knew I wasn't okay.

"Old Man Young gonna be fine, trust me," Everest said. "You know he strong as shit."

This bitch swears she knows me. Swears its okay to talk to me, even though I told her several times to leave me the fuck alone.

"Mad, Everest is talking to you," Gage said with an attitude. "You better speak to her because I know you want to."

Let me tell you about Gage, ever since I told her again I didn't want her touching me, she's been ignoring me. When we're in the cubby she doesn't speak to me. When we're around The Pit she doesn't talk to me. The only reason she's saying anything to me now is because she wants to prove her point that I'm attracted to Everest instead of her.

Ignoring everybody, I focused on the front of the Soup Kitchen when I saw three dudes standing in the doorway. They were hanging around, pointing and laughing at us while we ate our food.

When I looked toward my right I saw a mop. I walked over to it and untwisted the wooden handle from the rag part. When I was done I walked toward the entrance and whacked the first nigga over the head I could reach. The others ran but it doesn't bother me because all I need is one victim.

I could hear Spirit yelling behind me but I couldn't make out his words and I didn't care about what he was saying anyway. I didn't have plans to stop, until I saw the pearl color of his skull.

Blood splattered over my face, the ground, the walls, and the windows of the soup kitchen. When I looked down at his face I knew he was scared. I guess he didn't see this coming when he decided to fuck with us. He didn't know that I had been bullied all of my life and that my friend was just beaten probably to death. I'm about to kill him when I felt a hand on my shoulder. When I turned around I saw Father Brian, the priest who runs the kitchen. The moment he touched me I'm immediately at ease, and I realize what I did. Snapped.

Behind him are my friends, and they all looked scared. But Everest had a different look on her face that I can't explain. Maybe she understood why I went off. Maybe she understood why I needed to take out my anger on him.

"Madjesty, it's over," Father Brian said taking the bloody handle from my clenched hand. "You don't have to hurt this young man anymore."

How did he know my full name? I've never held a conversation with him a day in my life.

Instead of asking, I dropped the mop handle to the ground and when I looked down at my feet, the nigga I just tried to kill was gone.

Sirens went off in the background.

"Get out of here," Father Brian said calmly. "Before the police come. I'll take care of everything for you." When I don't move he yelled, "Go! Now!"

They didn't have to fuck right in the middle of The Crossroads. They could have gone to The Dump. But there they were, two West Wingers, fucking out in the open. I don't know what made it worse. The fact that I was with Pickles, or the fact that I hadn't fucked in weeks and was starting to hate myself for it.

Instead of cleaning Pickles up, I turned around to walk back to the cubby. When I made it there I was met with all members of Mad MaXXX. Their serious expressions let me know that something real was going on. Maybe they're mad at me about what happened earlier today at the soup kitchen. That shit could've gotten us all locked up. Since we're wanted. It was stupid and I regretted my move.

"What's up?" I asked, holding Pickles' hand tighter than I should have.

Spirit looked at Gage who rolled her eyes and walked away.

"Can somebody tell me what the fuck is up?" I asked.

"Gage put you out of her cubby today, man," Fierce said. "She said it ain't working, and she needs her space."

My heart punched my chest. "Put me out? For what? Because of what I did at the soup kitchen?"

"No," Everest said softly. "She said she doesn't like—"

"Shawty, why the fuck do you think I'm talking to you when I'm not?" I yelled in her face. "When I want to talk to you you'll know, until then step the fuck off."

Everest's lips trembled and she looked shocked. I guess now she knows how I really feel about her.

"Mad," Spirit said softly, "Everest didn't mean it that way. She was just trying to explain to you what's up because this shit is crazy. You and Gage were friends and now ya'll acting like enemies. So we don't know the real reason she put you out."

He was lying. He knew. He knew everything.

"Fierce, just take Pickles and Everest to my cubby," Spirit continued. "I'll be down in a minute after I rap to Mad."

He took Pickles away from me and already I felt empty. Spirited waited for them to disappear before he said anything.

"What's up, Spirit?" I asked. "I'm real confused."

"Mad, what is wrong with you lately?"

"Me," I pointed to myself. "What the fuck did I do?"

"For starters you been snapping at niggas left and right."

"What you talking about? The only time I say anything to anybody is when they're bothering me first."

"That's just it, nobody is bothering you. We trying to be there for you, but you won't let us. If you not out in the street drinking until you fall into a stupor, you fussing with us. You aren't the only one who feels bad about Old Man Young being in the hospital, but don't take it out on us. We family."

"Oh, so this is how ya'll try to be there for me, by putting me out? When you know I don't have no place else to go? And that I can't be up top or I'll get arrested for some shit I didn't do?"

"We going to set you up with your own cubby, Mad. Nobody is putting you out of the tunnel. We already got stuff for you and everything. If anything having your own spot down here may be what you need to get your mind right."

"So ya'll knew about this before the soup kitchen? That she was putting me out?"

"Yes."

I felt like punching him in the face. The next question I *wanted* to know more than I *needed* to know. I was just trying to find the right words to say that wouldn't make me feel like a punk. "Why, man? Be real with me because I know you know. If she not doing this because of how I snapped on dude at the soup kitchen, then why she doing it?"

He sighed. "Because she's in love with you, Mad." I could tell that was hard for him. It probably would be messed up for me too if I was feeling somebody who wasn't into me. "If you would calm down and see things for what they really are you would know that already. She already had her heart broken fucking with Wicked, and she can't take it anymore. And to tell you the truth, if I see her cry again, I don't know how I'm going to react."

I knew that was a threat and in my own way I respected it.

"You know what, if she wants to put me out that's on her. I'm tired of dealing with this chick anyway. But I do know this; her putting me out just proves that the only person I can count on is myself. And I'm good with that shit too."

CHAPTER 13

MAD

I'm glad Gage did that shit because it made me somewhat responsible. Since they put me up in my own cubby I decided I needed a job to get my spot together. The thing was, I couldn't get a job in the traditional sense because I'm wanted. In order for me to take care of myself what I really needed was a hustle. Spirit, Fierce and WB decided to help me with some ideas. And Gage and Everest tagged along even though I wasn't speaking to either of them.

The first thing I did was asked Fortune to watch Pickles. He liked hanging with her because she was good to him and he liked her dog, *Leave Me Alone*. After he was set I washed my face with some fresh bottled water, and then I set out to my first gig— collecting cans. I was excited the night before when Spirit and me went over the plan. If all I had to do was go through some trashcans to get some dough it wouldn't be a problem. I was focused.

We started dumping trashcans at seven o'clock in the morning and didn't finish until seven o'clock that night. I was tired and my feet ached so badly that when I was done I took my shoes off and my feet had swollen up so big I couldn't put them back on. The next morning we went to turn the bags of cans into the recycling company and I was fucked up when I saw what he was trying to pay me.

"What the fuck is this?" I asked the older Latino man behind the counter. Mad MaXXX along with Everest stood behind me looking just as confused.

"Money," he said rolling his eyes. "What the fuck it look like?"

"But we gave you five bags of cans," I told him while leaning on the counter. "I know you not trying to play me with one buck and some coins! You better come better than this shit."

"If that's what you call it, so be it."

I felt my face heat up. "I know one thing, you better give me the rest of my money."

"And if I don't?" he laughed. "Just what the fuck you plan to do little dyke?"

I looked back at my friends. "Please don't," Spirit whispered.

I guess he could tell by looking in my eyes that I was about to go for it. When the dude looked behind him and turned around, I stole him in the nose.

"You dyke bitch," he yelled trying to chase me. "I'm going to kill you!"

He really tried to catch me but it wasn't happening because I was already gone. I was so quick I left the money on the counter for the cans. FUCK! I know one thing; I'm done with that job.

After the *Can Gig* didn't go as planned I got fifteen CD's from a West Winger who was selling them for a dollar a piece. Spirit fronted me the money and I knew the job would be easy because they were already packaged and were from popular artists. We figured that although we bought them for a buck each, since we could sell them each for $10.00 we would make $150 if we stayed on our grind.

The shit worked too. Not only did we move them all, we did the shit in one day. When we got done we bought a bottle of liquor and ordered some pizzas. With the change I had left over I paid Spirit back and was able to get Pickles some new clothes and tennis shoes, which he always lost because he hated his toes covered. I was also able to get a case of water, some sheets and some more soap. I even gave Fierce a few bucks so that he would have some money for his meds. Just because I lived underground didn't mean I wanted to live nasty either.

We were up all night kicking it and I was feeling so good I even gave Gage and Everest eye contact even though I didn't speak to them. Shit was cool until the next day.

When we went back on the block I was told by three different people that some dudes were looking for us. I was chilling on the wall of the Korean store when an older white lady with a mean face came at me like she wanted to kill me.

She was wearing a red dress and a white baseball cap. I'm not sure how old she was but if I had to guess I'd say 65, give or take a gray hair.

"You the one that was selling them CD's the other day right?" she asked nicely even though she was frowning.

"Yeah," I said before looking back at Mad MaXXX who was leaning against the brick wall posing. Spirit shrugged, I guess not knowing where she was going with her line of questioning. "Why you asking?"

"Well I bought the TD Jakes CD from you. You remember that shit?"

"Oh yeah, I remember." I smiled. "I had a couple of those. I'm sold out now though. You wanted another one for someone else or something?"

She opened her mouth and a glob of warm hock spit came flying out and in my direction. It landed on my left eye and dampened my eyelash.

"The CD you gave me was blank, bitch! Take that!"

When she was done she stomped away. It took everything in my power not to yoke her, and punch her in the face.

I was mad as fuck while I wiped that shit off my eye. Mad MaXXX thought the shit was funny, while they spread out on the ground laughing. I punched the wall and almost broke my hand.

Later on that night I tried to catch up with the West Winger who sold me them fake CD's but he didn't come back to The Catacombs. I better never see him again that's for sure.

The next hustle we picked up was selling some girl socks we found in the trashcan of this department store that burned down a week earlier. They were pink and yellow with red hearts all over them. They were a little smoky smelling, but since they were putting them on their feet I didn't think it would be a problem.

I thought wrong. We spent the following night outside of the Korean store trying to sell just one pack of socks but people would look at us, roll their eyes and keep walking. Like we had them joints on our feet or something. In the end we got no love.

Frustrated, Gage threw the socks to the ground that were sitting inside of a white bucket, flipped the bucket over and started beating on top of it with her hands. I was surprised that she had a rhythm to her flow. If you closed your eyes she sounded like she was playing a drum.

Getting into mode, WB grabbed the two empty soda cans we were using earlier and started scraping them across the brick wall. In my opinion the shit started sounding real slick and went with Gage's drum sound. That's when Fierce started making this base noise from his mouth. It sounded like beat boxing but deeper. Everest got out in front of us and started dancing and that's when I saw how beautiful she really was. I knew even more in that moment that I had to stay away from her. She would be trouble for my heart, and I wasn't trying to risk it.

With everybody else in on the show. I started singing the lyrics of a song that always stuck in my head. I never sang before because I didn't have anything to sing about but the song reminded me of when my ex-girl Passion begged to be back with me and I didn't give her a chance. So I closed my eyes and let the lyrics flow.

♪ *'I left my girl back home…*
I don't love her no more…
But she'll never fucking know that….
These fucking eyes that I'm staring at… ♪

The song was called *Wicked Games* by a cat name *The Weekend*. I felt the lyrics to this song on a deep level, and I couldn't explain why.

I sang the whole song and when I opened my eyes after finishing, I noticed it was quiet and Mad MaXXX was staring at me. Did I do that bad? What really fucked me up was that we had a crowd of people around us, and the ground was littered with dollar bills. They literally sat at my feet and laid against my ankles. I zoned out and I didn't know what was happening around me.

A bunch of strangers gave me a round of applause and I almost shitted on myself when I saw a cop clapping too.

Instead of recognizing me, he dropped a ten-dollar bill and walked off.

When the cop disappeared down the block I said, "What happen?" I took one last look to be sure he wasn't coming back.

"Mad, why you ain't tell us you could sing?" Spirit asked. "You killed it!"

"Because I can't." I frowned.

"Well you better tell your voice that shit because it don't know."

━━━━━━━━●━━━━━━━━━━━━━━━━━━━━━━━━━━●━━━━━━━━

We were in Spirit's place, drinking Hennessey and eating Popeye's Chicken. We made one hundred and seventy seven dollars that night. We divided the cash up and after they told me how good I sang, which I didn't want to keep hearing, Everest jumped up to take the mike. I was just getting ready to like the bitch again.

"...And really Rome is much more beautiful than China," Everest said while she stood in the middle of the floor. "You all have to see it."

We weren't even talking about Rome.

"You been to Rome?" Gage asked as she stared at her as if she were the Statue of Liberty. "Was it as spectacular as in my dreams?"

"Better. I kissed the ground of the coliseum and everything. I will never forget it in my life." She would look at me every time she'd say something. I guess because she was trying to impress me even though I wasn't buying her shit. Why she got to be so extra? One minute she would be cool, and the next minute she was annoying.

"So what about China," Spirit asked. "How did it look when you went? Because I always wanted to know about that side of my family, but I never had an opportunity to go."

Her eyes lit up. "You'd love it, Spirit. It's very crowded but..."

I decided that I had enough of her mouth so I walked out. I went to The Pit and drank my Hennessey in peace. Fifteen minutes later she came outside with me. In my heart I knew she would do it.

"You don't believe me do you? That I went to the places I claimed I'd been? You can tell me, I can take it."

I stared at the fire. "Even if I don't believe you why should you care? You don't owe me nothing, shawty." I took another swig of Hennessey.

"Mad, I'm really a nice person if you would just get to know me. I just wish I could do something to convince you of that."

I laughed." It don't matter if you a nice person or not because like I said, I'm not interested in you or your fake ass adventures. Now kick rocks, I'm thinking right now and you blowing me."

She whipped out something small and blue from her back pocket. It had gold letters on the front and she handed it to me. "That's my passport. If you don't believe me look inside of it."

Curious I flipped through the first page.

"Read all of the stamps, Mad," she continued. "They'll show you where I've been. I'm not lying."

I looked down at the thing in my hand and it could've been in Greek because I couldn't read too well. The only word I knew was China. "Here, I don't want this shit." I tried to hand it back to her but she wouldn't accept it.

"No, I want you to read it first," she smiled.

"I said no," I yelled. "Now stepped the fuck off, because you bothering me!" I dropped it on the ground.

She looked at me crazily at first, and then her facial expression softened. "You can't read can you?"

My scalp felt like it tightened and my temples throbbed. This was beyond embarrassing. "That's your fucking problem. You don't know what to say out your mouth. But I'm warning you to stay the fuck away from me," I pointed in her face. "I once hurt a girl just like you for similar shit and she ain't on the earth anymore." I walked away.

CHAPTER 14
MAD

We decided to have a barbeque because despite the beating they put on him, Old Man Young had returned. The fucked up part is I'm not in the mood to celebrate. Somebody stole some shit out of my cubby and I knew it was Wicked. The dude had been extra quiet lately and it wasn't like him not to say something at least once each day. The worst part about it was that I needed the money to get Pickles some cold medicine since he was sick. I guess the damp temperature in The Catacombs finally caught up with him.

The thievery shit messed my head up and I was looking for the right time to go on my own again up top, like I usually did whenever I got in this mood. The only thing was that now I had Pickles, and people got so use to me looking after him, that I had to care for him solo. Pickles really doesn't like when I bounce.

The other day I was gone for one day and when I came back they told me how he was crying nonstop, thinking that I wasn't going to come back like his parents. I don't want to be responsible for his heart.

To make shit wetter last night I had a dream about my mother. She was standing in the kitchen with a blank look on her face. On the counter next to the stove where she stood was a big green lizard with red eyes. He kept staring at me like he wanted to kill me. There was also a pan on the stove, and inside of it was a whole apple.

I was sitting at the table where two cracked eggs sat in front of me. And when I looked down at the floor maple syrup was everywhere.

I don't know what the dream was about, but it fucked with my head, and all I wanted was some Hennessey to get her out of my mind. But since my money was stolen, and the group cash we stashed needed to be shared with six to seven people, I was broke.

I decided to go to my room, but first I walked over to Old Man Young's cubby. I needed to kick it with him for a second in private before the party. "I'm glad you're back, man," I said when I saw him sitting on his bed reading a book. A black eye patch covered the place where one of his eyes use to be.

"Thank you," he said looking up at me. "Are you okay?" he slammed the book closed and placed it down next to him. "You seem troubled."

I pulled my cap down, and stuffed my hands into my jean pockets. "It's nothing I can't work out. Anyway this day is about you."

"It wasn't the first time I was beaten within every inch of my life, and it probably won't be the last."

I thought about what he said earlier, when he first got back. He said he forgave the dudes that beat him and that it was more important to move on with his life, and I couldn't get with that. It seemed weak to me. "How come you acting like it never happened? Like them niggas never banked your ass. I don't get it."

"Because I refuse to let them take anymore of my time. I'm alive, and it must mean God has work for me to do. And I'm going to do it."

"That's easier said than done."

"For some," he smiled. "But not for me. You see when you hold onto hate for so long, it does more damage to you than anybody else physically. It eats at your insides, and that's how you find yourself with cancers and all other kinds of things you can't explain."

"But you got cirrhosis of the liver," I reminded him.

"Yeah, but I know how I got it too. That was from good old fashion liquor drinking. I'm talking about people who find themselves with cancer and other illnesses they can't explain. The way I live life is like this. I don't stress over anything I can't change. And even though I got cirrhosis, I'm not dead yet and I contribute that to my positive outlook on life."

If you ask me he sounded dumb but I didn't tell him that. If somebody would've done some shit like that to me, I would want them dead and I would make sure it happened too. "That's good to hear," I said sarcastically, "I'll rap to you later."

After saying goodbye I walked toward my room. I guess it was a good thing Gage put me out because now I could spend some time alone to figure things out. Well, at least that's what I wanted to do until I heard Pickle's feet slapping behind me.

When we made it to my room I climbed into bed, wanting to get some sleep. But Pickles picked up his book like he was about to read me a story again.

"Not now, lil man. I want to get some rest."

He coughed. "But I wanted to read—"

"Lil man, go back out to The Pit if you want to read," I said louder. "Right now I want to be alone."

He dropped his book and stormed out. I felt bad but I'm being real with him. I was about to go to sleep until WB walked in. "You got a second, man?"

I sighed. "Not really. I just wanted to—"

"I'm thinking about detoxing, Mad, and I don't know what to do." He sat on the only chair I had.

I sat up and looked over at him. I figured if I spoke to him he would leave me alone. "So what's the problem? Go detox."

"I don't want to leave ya'll behind. And what if I'm a different person when I get back? You know? Or what if ya'll not here no more and I don't have anything to return to?"

"WB, you gotta do what's good for you." I tugged my cap. "If you got a chance to kick your habit you should go ahead and do it, man. I mean, I would give up this bottle in a minute."

"You would?"

"I would."

"So why don't you do it?"

That was a serious question I didn't give a lot of thought to before I said it. Even with Old Man Young telling me that I should cut some shit back because of my urinary tract, in my mind he didn't know what he was talking about. I liked my liquor and that was the bottom line. I wasn't like him. I just wanted to drink because I could.

"Because I don't want to," I told him. "But look, man, I'm about to get some sleep. Do me a favor, Pickles is mad with me right now. Can you keep an eye on him while he's out there?"

"You know I got him."

He gave me some dap and walked out. I was just about to shut my eyes again when I felt somebody else in my room. The presence was so dark it scared me. When I turned around I was looking at Wicked. And the look he gave me could kill.

CHAPTER 15
MAD

See this is the kind of shit that made me hate this dude. Instead of leaving me the fuck alone he gotta pull ignorant moves. I'm in my room trying to get some sleep, when out of the blue Wicked comes in claiming I stole his money. He even had some West Wingers with him that said they saw me walk out of his room. And because I left The Pit early and didn't have anybody but WB to vouch for me it looked bad.

And now I'm standing in front of Old Man Young and The Parable trying to prove my innocence. I swear if I had somewhere else to go I wouldn't care. The problem with Wicked lying was that if they found me guilty, then I could be asked to leave. Although The Catacombs belonged to no one, they would make shit hard for anybody who stayed against their will.

No one would talk to you, which I wouldn't care. You would have to stay in your cubby because every time you'd leave the power would be disconnected and they would trash your place. In the end it wasn't worth it to defy the laws, but just go with the flow.

"Mad, as you know we take things seriously down here," Old Man Young said. "And as a member of The Catacombs you are essentially surrendering to our laws. Correct?"

"I guess," I responded tugging at my baseball cap.

"Well then...we are here to discuss what happened to Wicked's money. Did you or did you not steal it?"

"I did not," I said as I stood with my hands clasped behind me. I was trying my best not to use them to choke Wicked out. I didn't need this shit right now. "And when my money was stolen I didn't come to ya'll about it. I took it as a loss."

"Well you shouldn't have," The Parable said. "We would've held a meeting and—"

"What?" I asked cutting him off. "Just what would you have done? Nothing," I yelled. "For all I know this dude stole my money and then went to ya'll first so I would look bad if I said something. This whole situation is weak."

"I ain't steal shit from you, cuz," Wicked responded with a smirk on his face.

Yeah, he got me for my money.

"WB can vouch that I was in my cubby today."

"We decided not to allow WB's testimony because he is your friend and may lie for you."

"That's bullshit," I said pacing the small place in front of me.

"I'm sorry you feel that way," Old Man Young said. "And although we have warned you all against leaving money in your spaces, we would've at least investigated the matter. But you didn't come to us. Today we're here on Wicked's business."

I gritted my teeth. I hate these funky mothafuckas.

"Wicked, what proof do you have that Mad stole your money?" the Parable asked him.

"My man Daze right here said he saw her."

"Sir, if it is true that WB can't vouch for Mad and say that he was with her at the time this money was supposedly stolen, then Daze shouldn't be allowed to testify for Wicked either," Everest interjected in my defense.

For the first time ever I was feeling her. And it wasn't because of how she looked defending me, but that she decided to say anything at all.

Old Man Young whispered to The Parable. When he was done he looked back at Wicked. "She's right. Unless you have another witness we don't have any reason to believe she did it."

I tried to hide the smile on my face. It wasn't because I was pressed to live here. Naw, that wasn't it at all. It was the fact that no matter what this dude did to try to fuck with me nothing worked in his favor.

"What the fuck is up with everybody in this bitch?" Wicked yelled. "Why do you show loyalty to her when she doesn't deserve it? Huh? I've been here longer than her, but none of ya'll act like it matters. What about the loyalty?"

"We've said our piece," The Parable said before leaving.

"I'm going to hit you where it hurts," Wicked said to me.

Everyone else walked away including him. But his voice echoed in my mind long after he was gone. I knew I was going to have to find another place to stay or we were going to come to deadly blows.

●━━━━━━━━━━━━━━━━━━━━━●

Every now and again somebody in the crew had to go shoplift for food if money wasn't coming in. This time it was my turn. I had all intentions on going by myself, but Blazer and Motor Angel from the West wanted to come with me because I found some bus passes. Spirit told me not to take them, but they kept begging and promised to stay away from me in the store if I let them.

Blazer was a scrawny kid who was real tall with skin darker than WB's. He didn't say much but when he did he was asking for food and money. Motor Angel was okay to look at, but I didn't give her too much attention because she always read into things the wrong way. She'd brush up to me at The Pit and ask to lick my pussy, which I hated. No matter what she did or said I couldn't get up with her.

When we got off of the bus I put it down to them straight. "Listen, don't follow me and I won't follow you in the store. Get what you going to get and when you're done I'll meet you around the back. That way we can divide up everything we got. Cool?"

Blazer rubbed his nose so hard it started bleeding. "I got you," he said wiping the blood off with the back of his hand. "I won't be no trouble I appreciate the pass."

Disgusted I walked through the aisles on a mission. I skillfully placed can good after can good in my backpack, and was moving toward the candy aisle to cop some stuff for Pickles. We couldn't afford candy all of the time but since he liked it so much, I went a few times without getting a bottle of Hennessey for my man. The bottle was the only reason I was able to get up each day, so I knew I fucked with the kid more than I wanted to admit.

I stuffed a pack of Twizzlers in my bag when through the corner of my eyes, I saw a beefy white man walking behind Motor Angel and Blazer. The man had his hands on their shoulders and I already knew what was going down. They were caught.

FUCK!

My shopping trip was officially over and I hustled toward the exit. But that's when the illest shit happened. The nigga Blazer actually said, "That girl dressed like a boy over there is with us too."

When I turned around his ashy finger was pointing in my direction. I felt like unleashing on him but first I had to get out of the store without being arrested. This shit was do or die for me. If I got caught, I was going to be held up and the cops would find out that I was wanted for the murder of Rose Midland.

When I reached the door another black man stood in front of me and pushed me to the floor. He snatched the backpack from my hand and opened it.

He dug his hand inside, grabbed a can of green beans and said, "Well, well, well, what do we have here you, little thief?"

I'm sitting in some office in the grocery store with one hand cuffed to the table. Motor Angel was crying, they had one wrist cuffed too. Blazer was trying not to look at us. I don't know where the two men went who arrested us, but I'm sure at any moment they'll be coming back with the police.

"I'm sorry about this shit, Mad," Blazer said. "I didn't—"

"Nigga, don't say shit else to me," I told him slamming my fist on the table. "You snitched and from where I'm from the penalty is death."

There was no other sound in the room with the exception of Motor Angel's sniffling. When the door opened a woman I recognized came walking into the room. I didn't know where I knew her from, but she definitely looked familiar.

"Before I call the police," she said sitting down and looking at Blazer, "I want to know what you three were doing stealing in my store? I take thieves very seriously around here."

She looked at Motor Angel and then at me. But the look on her face turned from anger to something different. "It's you," she said pointing at me. "You're the one."

My heart pounded and I felt like every part of my skin itched. She recognized me from the Wanted ad that was going around DC. "You know me?"

"Of course I do," she smiled. "You helped my son on the train. You defended him when those guys came in and scared him. I thought we were going to die. Don't you remember? I never got a chance to say thank you, because you ran away when you saw the cops."

Oh snap! That was her. I'm not going to lie; at the moment I was relieved although I knew it would be short lived. After all, I would still be going to jail because at the end of the day I did steal some shit.

"It wasn't nothing," I shrugged.

Suddenly she stood up and uncuffed my wrist. "Follow me."

I rubbed my arm where the bracelet use to be and looked at Blazer and Motor Angel before I followed her into the hallway. "What's up?" I leaned against the wall and pulled down my baseball cap.

"I'm going to let you go," she said the moment the door closed.

I leaned in. "F-f-for real?" I stuttered.

"Yes," she smiled. "I'm the general manager here and it would be my honor to return the favor to you. You don't understand what you did for me that day. I can tell something was going on with you, and you didn't have to help me but you did. I am eternally grateful for you. Always."

I stood up straight. "But how can you let me go? I mean, won't you get in trouble?"

"Don't worry about all of that," she looked around. "Just know that if I do this you can never come back here. Ever."

"Lady, if you let me go you don't ever have to worry about me walking back up in this bitch again," I said eager to run away. "That's on my life."

To make things even better she dug into her pocket and handed me a one hundred dollar bill. My eyes lit up and I was thrown off. All of my life I was use to adults taking advantage of me or not giving a fuck but she was different.

"That's for you. I don't know what had you feeling like you needed to steal, but I hope that eases some of the pressure. Now get out of here before somebody sees you. Go out the back door." She pointed behind me at the exit.

I was about to roll out but I thought about Blazer and Motor Angel. A part of me wanted to say fuck them, but I wasn't built like that. I didn't want to see them in jail.

"What about them," I pointed to the door.

"What about them?" She frowned. "From what I heard they sold you up the creek, and told the officers that you do stuff like that all of the time. They thought by selling you out that they'd get a better deal or something." She laughed to herself and shook her head. "They are going to get exactly what they deserve. Locked up."

Just thinking about Blazer's lanky finger pointing in my direction made me want to agree but I didn't want to do it like that. "I know, but do you think you could help them out? It would mean a lot to me. They don't have no honor code, but I do."

She shook her head and smiled at me again. "I can tell by the way you beat that kid on the bus that you been through a lot, but I can also tell you have a good heart too. I don't know why but I got a feeling that you're going to be okay in life, just give it some time."

"I appreciate that, ma'am, but people like me don't get breaks. It's not in the cards for us."

"So what do you call what I just did for you?"

CHAPTER 16
MAD

Today we had another barbeque and I couldn't keep my eyes off of Everest for some reason. She was wearing tight jeans and a cute red top that hugged her breasts. I haven't fucked in a long time so I was overdue but her and I wouldn't work.

As we stood around The Pit, and I watched her laugh and talk to Mad MaXXX suddenly I could see why they liked her so much. Something told me to stay away from her, but it was getting harder to do.

"What's wrong with you, man?" I asked Spirit who seemed grumpy. "You acting like me today."

"It's Fierce, man."

I looked over at Fierce who was kicking it with WB and Fortune. "What he do this time? Not take his medicine or something?"

"You know how I am about leaving open food in the cubby and shit right? So I told him when he stayed the night over to make sure that he threw any trash outside of my cubby. Instead of listening this nigga goes to sleep and then look"— he lowered his head and pointed at the hair on his Mohawk— "Do you see that shit, man?"

"What you talking about?" I asked examining the crown of his head.

"What am I talking about? Look at my fucking hair" he moved his head closer like it would make me see something differently. "Because he left food and drink all over my cubby the rats came inside and started chewing at my hair. Fuck!" He raised his head and rubbed his Mohawk.

I tried not to smile but it didn't work. I was laughing so hard I held onto my stomach. Just picturing rats on top of his head was hilarious. "My bad, man," I said trying to calm down. "I don't mean to be laughing it's just that—,"

"Fuck you," Spirit said shaking his head. "Anyway, what's up with Blazer and Motor Angel? They been staying away ever since ya'll got back from the grocery store. Something happen?"

When we got back, after the snitch fest at the store. I didn't tell about the way Blazer pointed the finger at me, and how Motor Angel was with it. The only thing I said was that the plan to cop from that grocery store didn't work, and that I went to another spot on my own. I brought food back to my team from the one hundred dollar bill the lady gave me. So we were good.

I guess Blazer and Motor Angel thought I said something and hid in shame. Fuck them niggas.

"I'm not their keeper so you gotta ask them where they be," I frowned.

"I got fresh bread," WB said walking into The Pit area. Behind him was Fortune who never left his side.

We all walked over to him. "Where you get it from?" Gage asked excitedly. "I can eat some more even though I'm full."

"From the back of a bakery," he responded. "Don't worry, though it's clean."

Clean to them meant that the bread was thrown in a bag by itself, without other trash. I hated food from cans and unlike my crew; I refused to eat anything like that.

So instead of saying anything I said, "Well I'm going to the store to grab a bottle. I'll be back in a second. Anybody want anything?"

"Can I go with you?" Everest asked me.

Damn this bitch pretty. "Did I ask you to come with me?"

"No," she said sadly.

"Fortune, keep an eye on Pickles for me," I said.

"You know I got my baby," she smiled.

When I walked down the East Wing and outside of the tunnel to get my liquor, my heart stopped when I saw the person in front of me. She was still beautiful. Her long black hair hung down her back and not a piece of hair was out of place. The pink sweater she wore made her cleavage spill out of her shirt. She was sexy, real sexy, but what was she doing here?

I hadn't seen her since she was in my grandmother's, on my father's side, basement. It was because of me that she was tied up and put down there by my father as a hostage.

It was long ago but I still remember. She was in the nail salon when my father sent me inside to lure her out. I tried to pretend that I was selling her some cookies so that I could go to college. She wouldn't buy it though, and in the end I faked a seizure. When I fell out on the floor, I told her that my father was outside in the car and that I needed my medicine. She walked out there to get him and he used the opportunity to hit her over the head and throw her in the backseat. Afterwards he took her to his mother's house and kept her in the basement. So what was she doing here?

I looked around her to see if she was with the cops or anybody else…like my father. She represented the past. Both the good and bad times.

"How did you find me?" I asked pulling my cap down over my eyes.

"It wasn't hard."

"Well if it wasn't hard just tell me."

She stood at the entrance of The Catacombs unafraid, even though she looked out of place. "I've been searching the shelters and soup kitchens for you. And finally I saw you one day outside of one of the kitchens beating a kid with a mop handle. I followed you and your friends and that's how I ended up here"— she looked at the entrance of the tunnel behind me as if she was seeing it for the first time— "how could you live in a place like this?"

I frowned. Who the fuck is she to come at me like that? "What you mean?"

"You are living in a tunnel, Madjesty. Where rats and dirty sewer water pours. How could you reduce yourself to such conditions?" She looked at my hair and then my face. "The cleanest thing on you is your shoes, which look new by the way."

"Where's my father?" I said, trying to convince myself not to hurt her.

Outside of Wicked, I didn't have anybody telling me I wasn't good enough and it didn't feel good hearing it from her.

"That's what I wanted to talk to you about. He's looking for you. He's been looking for you ever since he found out you were wanted for killing that girl." She paused. "Did you do it?"

"No."

A part of me deep inside felt better that my pops cared. The fact that anybody gave a fuck about me outside of my family in The Catacombs made me feel worthy. Made me feel blessed.

Blessed?

Wow.

I never used that word before.

Although I thought about my life on the outside I had to face the fact that I was wanted for murder, and because of it I couldn't leave The Catacombs.

"Did he say what he wanted?"

"For you to go with him. He's not safe in the DMV anymore either, Mad. A lot of shit has gone down and Kali isn't sure if he still has beef with friends of your sister's father. As you know before Jace died of HIV, Kali had been trying to kill him."

"Jace is dead?" I asked in a low voice.

"Yes, you didn't know?"

I shook my head. "No...I mean...how is Jayden?"

Just saying my sister's name caused my stomach to rumble.

"I don't know, I'm not interested in her. I'm here about you. Now are you coming with me so that I can get Kali out of town or not? He's not listening to me about how dangerous things are here. He's waiting on you. So let's go, Mad."

I looked behind me into the deep darkness of the tunnel. Where rats, vagrants, killers, and every other horrible thing you could imagine roamed. With all that said, as of right now The Catacombs was my home.

I looked back at her. "I can't go, I'm sorry."

She frowned. "Why not?"

"Because until I can figure out what I'm going to do about this murder I didn't do, I can't leave. Not even with my father."

She rolled her eyes.

Fuck this bouige ass bitch.

"I'm offering you an escape. It's not like it's different from what you're doing here. At least there you'll be safe and clean."

"I can't."

"Well I'm going to ask you one more thing," she said.

"What?"

"To stay away from him. I'm going to tell Kali that you are gone for good, and I'm going to convince him to go back with me to Atlanta. I don't want you reaching out to him. I need you to stay out of his life. Can you do that? Please."

I thought about what she was saying. Who was she to tell me when or how I talked to my father? I could tell she loved him though.

"You got my word. You can tell him that I'm dead, and I'll never bother him."

CHAPTER 17
MAD

I've been in the drunk zone for the past few days. Ever since Antoinette came over and told me my father was looking for me. I felt wrong for agreeing to do what she wanted. I don't know if I made the right decision. Maybe it would have given me a better chance to stay out of jail and get my son. Even if I wanted to change my mind I don't have any way to get in contact with her. I fucked up.

When I walked down the East Wing toward the Crossroads, I heard Motor Angel and Blazer having sex again. Although I usually get mad, this time I stayed and watched. Motor Angel was leaned against the wall while Blazer had her off of her feet. Her legs wrapped around his waist. I was horny so I stuffed my hand down my pants to rub my joint.

I'm filled with anger and pleasure at the same time. I'm mad that I haven't fucked in a minute, and even angrier that I was about to rub off to two people I couldn't stand. I really hit bottom. I took my hands out of my pants.

I was just about to go to my room and drink the rest of my bottle when I heard Pickle's voice. I hadn't seen him in about two days because I needed to be alone. Fortune, Gage and Everest took care of him, giving me the space I needed to think. As far as I knew he was supposed to be with them now, so what was he doing down here in the darkness?

Because it was so black down here and I couldn't see down the hall where he was, so I just listened. "Please leave me alone," Pickles said again.

I felt chill bumps rise up on my skin. What the fuck was happening to my little man? When I moved closer toward his voice I saw Wicked's white skin. He was pulling Pickles pants down. I lost it. At least that's what it felt like.

I rushed up to Wicked, stole him in the face and slammed him against the wall. He had something in his hand that resembled a knife and was about to stab me until Pickles yelled. "Help, please!"

Immediately Motor Angel and Blazer stopped fucking and rushed over toward us. Right behind them was Spirit, Gage, WB, Fierce and Everest.

"What's going on," Spirit asked looking at me, Wicked and Pickles.

By this time The Crossroads was filled with everyone who lived there. I guess they were trying to figure out what the fuck was going on too.

"This nigga was doing something to Pickles." I pulled Pickles behind me to protect him from Wicked. "And I caught him. I thought you were supposed to be watching him, man?"

"I'm sorry, I…we had a dope bag and—"

"You wasn't watching him," I yelled. "This dude was about to rape my man."

Everybody gasped and looked at him.

"This bitch is lying," Wicked said, as his eyes moved quickly from left to right. He was off that heroin. I could tell.

"I wouldn't lie on my enemy about something like that." I said. "Even you." I focused back on everybody else.

"This mothafucka *was* just messing with Pickles. If you don't believe me ask him."

"First off I believe you," Spirit said. "But I want everybody else to believe you too." He bent down in front of Pickles who was shivering. "Pickles, how you doing, lil man?"

"I'm fine," he said wiping his face with the back of his hand.

"That's good, that's real good"— Spirit looked up at me and then back at him— "Can you tell me what happened just now?"

Pickles was quiet.

"Tell them, lil man," I said looking down at him, "don't worry about Wicked. I won't let him hurt you again." I meant that shit.

"Like you could stop me if I wanted to hurt him," Wicked said preparing to approach us.

"If you take another step you gonna get a glimpse of my past and what I'm capable of." He stopped in his tracks. "Don't let this curly hair fool you."

Spirit focused back on Pickles. "Did he hurt you, Pickles?"

Pickles cried softly.

"Answer him, lil man," I said. I couldn't lie I was getting frustrated with Pickles. Why was he scared when I told him he was safe? "Everything is going to be okay. Talk to Uncle Spirit."

"Did he do anything to you, Pickles?" Spirit asked. He sounded annoyed. "It's okay, you can tell me."

Pickles looked up at me, Spirit and everyone else. I knew he was scared and all I wanted to do was take him away from everything. I wanted to take him away from his problems.

When he was finally ready to talk in the lightest voice he said, "No, sir, he didn't bother me. He didn't bother me at all."

My little man failed me.

Damn.

CHAPTER 18
MAD

Pickles sat on the edge of my bed holding onto his favorite book *Cinderella*. I knew what the book said because last week Spirit asked him why does he like Cinderella so much, since he makes up his own stories anyway. That's the one thing I regret more than anything, not learning as much as I could in school. I guess it wouldn't make a difference if someone like me knew how to read because I'll never amount too much in life anyway.

As I watched Pickles play with the pages of the book, I really wanted to talk to him about what happened with Wicked. I needed him to know that I was there for him and even though I was mad I still fucked with him. I also wanted to tell him that I was sorry that I was too drunk to look after him and that if he trusted me again. I would never let him down.

Instead I said, "Pickles, how you doing?"

"Can I read you a story?" he asked looking up at me with his big brown eyes.

I sighed. The book shit was blowing me especially since I was trying to have a conversation with him. "You can read me a story after you tell me how you are."

In a low voice he said, "I want to read you a story first. Can I please?"

Hoping that after he finished, he would tell me how he felt I said, "Go 'head, lil man, afterwards we gotta talk though. About some real shit. Okay?"

He lit up. He pushed the book open and started spitting out words I'm sure were not in the book. "Once upon a time lived a little boy. He was sad most of the time but nobody liked him. One day a man he didn't like took him away. And he tried to…he tried too…"

As Pickles' words drifted off I understood what he was doing. He was trying to tell me what happened in his own way.

"…And then his friend came and saved him when the man pulled his pants down. The little boy was scared when his friend asked him what happened because he thought the man would hurt her. The little boy's friend looked sad and he hoped she wasn't mad at him. The end."

He slammed the book closed and looked up at me. Tears filled his eyes and I decided that he told me all I needed to know.

"That was a good one, little man. The realest story I ever heard."

"Thank you."

———•———————————————————•———

I was watching Pickles play with Spirit at The Pit. WB was over in The Dump shooting up. I guess his detox dreams were over which was fucked up. I was for anybody dropping something that's holding them back.

Since that shit happened with Pickles and Wicked, I kept a closer eye on him at all times. As a matter of fact I was still focusing on him when Everest walked up to me.

"You're good to him," she said. "I like that."

I tried not to look into her pretty face. "Thanks I guess."

"Can I talk to you in private?"

I focused on her eyes. "What you gotta talk to me in private for? We don't have no business together."

"Please, Mad, just for a second."

Although I knew I needed to be away from her I was also curious about what she wanted. So I walked over to Spirit and said, "Keep an eye on him."

"Don't worry, I got him."

"I'm serious, man. If Wicked gets his hands on him again I'm not going to be right. You got me? I'll be on some violent shit."

He swallowed. "I got you, man. Pickles is safe with me."

Me and Everest walked back into the tunnel but hung out in The Crossroads. "What's up, Everest?"

Instead of answering me, she kissed me in the mouth. I was about to push her back but she pulled me closer.

When she was done she said, "How do you feel?"

My tongue felt numb because the kiss made me high. What kinda game was she playing? I hadn't given her one bit of attention. "What the fuck was that about?" I wiped her kiss off even though it tasted like sugar.

"How do you feel?" she repeated.

"Man, I don't have time for this shit." I tried to walk around her but she blocked me.

"Mad, don't leave," she said standing in front of me grabbing my hand. "I'm not trying to disrespect you but I've been feeling you for awhile. You wouldn't believe how long it took me to pump myself up just to do that. And now that I…"

"I don't know why you playing yourself, Everest," Gage said walking up behind us. "Mad ain't interested in her friends." She looked at me. "Didn't she tell you? Because she sure did tell me."

"I didn't know you were over there, Gage," Everest said. "I thought—"

Gage slapped her in the face so hard Everest stumbled backwards into the wall. Everest touched her face where she'd just been hit.

"Gage, what the fuck is up with you?" I asked grabbing her by the wrist. "Why would you hit that girl?"

She frowned. "She knew how I felt about you and this is what she does? Disrespects me by going at you? I'm done with her. I'm done with everybody." Gage stomped away toward The Pit and Everest took one more look at me and then followed her.

Instead of going back outside I walked to my cubby to grab a bottle of Hennessy. But when I got there, I saw Fierce inside of my room. He was stealing from me.

CHAPTER 19
MAD

"I don't understand why you played me like this, Fierce," I said shoving him into the wall of my cubby. "Especially after everything I do for you."

"I know, I know," he said moving around my room. "But you gotta understand what I need on a regular basis ain't at no liquor store. This shit be calling me, Mad, and I need it everyday."

"And what the fuck is that?"

"Crack," he said in a low voice. "I'm on that new shit now. With each puff I take my problems go away."

The nigga sounded dumb.

"Tell the truth," I said breathing heavily. "You the one who been stealing from me all along?"

He looked guilty.

"Yes."

"You been stealing from Wicked too?"

He nodded yes.

"Do you realized the war you started between me and that dude? He got at Pickles and I know it had to do with him thinking I stole from him."

"I'm sorry," he said weakly.

"After everything I did for you, Fierce? That ain't just foul, nigga, that's dead." I wanted to hurt him so badly that the veins in my forehead pulsated.

"Mad, please don't get angry with me. I just—"

When he moved to touch me I pushed him back. He fell to the floor and stood up. "Get the fuck up out my room, nigga."

"Mad, don't—"

"Now," I yelled pointing at my door.

When he walked toward the door I sat on the edge of my bed and grabbed my bottle. I downed most of it and then looked out ahead of me. I can't believe he would play me like this. That goes to show that it don't matter who you think you know because at the end of the day you don't know shit.

While I was trying to get my mind right this dude name Fuzzy from the Apple Kings of the West Wing came busting through the door. "You want some cake, man?"

He had a piece of yellow cake in his bare hand and was holding it like a bitch. What the fuck I look like eating cake from this dude's palm? "Fuzzy, turn back around and get out, man. I got too much shit on my mind right now and somebody might get hurt."

"Oh...I was just asking 'cause—"

"Bounce," I screamed.

When he left I decided to take a nap. Actually I don't even think it was my decision. It just happened. One minute I was angry and the next minute I was drifting off to sleep. When I woke up about an hour later, I was dripping in sweat. Because my mother came to me again in my dreams and it fucked me up.

In the nightmare, I was in the bed at the shelter we lived in back in the day. She kept walking up to me throwing things on my bed. The first thing she threw on me was red grapes. I put the white sheet over my head because although they were grapes, it felt like she was flinging rocks instead. The next thing she threw on me was a bunch of green frogs. They were making loud noises in my ear and were really slimy. The next thing she threw at me was a dead owl. But the moment it hit my sheet it jumped up and flew away.

After sometime she went away and then a girl who use to be with us in the shelter in Texas, brought me a box of valentine candy in red heart box. She asked me to be her boyfriend and for some reason I said yes even though when I ate the candy it tasted like ice. I told her I changed my mind about being with her, and that I didn't like her anymore and she kept saying she would '*never ever speak to me again*'. As she walked away from the bed the only thing she kept saying was *ever*. I was still listening to her say the word *ever* until she walked out of sight.

I tried to get the crazy dream out of my mind so I got up and downed half of my Hennessy. Why the fuck was I dreaming about my mother?

When Everest came into my room I was irritated. "What do you want now?"

"Can we talk?"'

"Everest, I can appreciate the fact that you like me. But I don't do well with all of this drama you bringing. Ya'll gotta—"

"Why are you afraid to love me?" she asked stepping into my room. "It's so obvious that you fighting against me."

"Afraid to love you?" I chuckled. "What the fuck you talking 'bout? You don't know shit about me or who I love. Plus I'm not thinking anything about you." I looked away from her. "You not my type."

"You're going to be mine, Mad. Mark my words. And when you do you're going to be happy and wonder what took you so long to let me love you. Trust me. I'm a catch," she grinned.

This bitch was tripping. I was about to tell her when Mad MaXXX came into my room, minus the thieving nigga Fierce. Spirit, WB, and Gage stood in front of me and Fortune was with them holding Pickles' hand.

"What the fuck happen with, Fierce?" Spirit asked me.

"Ask him," I said refusing to tell them about what he tried to do.

"Then why he storm out like that?"

"I'm not his keeper and I'm not his friend either."

WB stepped up and said, "We'll get into that later. You need to be careful, Mad." At first I thought he was threatening me until he said, "Pop Kill is back."

"Who the fuck is a Pop Kill?"

"He's a murderer and he's also one of Wicked's closest friends. Word around The Catacombs is that Wicked's mad that you called him a child molester."

"That's cause he is a child molester," I told him.

"Pop Kill is asking for you," WB continued. "He said he wanted to meet you and when he says that it ain't never good."

CHAPTER 20
MAD

We were in The Pit and Fortune and Everest were dancing next to the fire. It's just the right temperature outside tonight...not too hot and not too cold. I was sharing a bottle of Henny with Spirit and everything felt peaceful. A little too peaceful if you asked me and I knew it was just a matter of time before something kicked off.

Fierce walked up to me. "Can I talk to you for a second, Mad?"

I looked around him like he wasn't on earth and remained silent.

"Mad, please," he said coughing a few times.

Silence.

"I know you aren't talking to me but I still want you to know that I'm sorry. I betrayed your trust and everything you did for me and I will never do that again. Ever."

Silence.

He walked away and out of The Pit.

It took me twenty minutes to relax after he left. I hate when people fuck up and expect you to accept their apologies so quickly. If I do decide to bring dude back into my life it's going to be on my time. Besides, he asked me five other times to be cool with him and each time I said no. So why ask me again?

I was staring at Everest move her waist from left to right, as she eye fucked me, when Spirit asked, "You like her huh?"

I repositioned my eyes on Fortune instead. I didn't want him to know that Everest was weighing on me. "Who you talking about? Fortune?"

"Fuck no," he laughed. "Everybody knows she belongs to WB. Stop fucking around, nigga and answer the question."

I laughed when I thought about what I said. I wasn't hardly attracted to her. Fortune belonged to WB, even if he didn't want her. The only reason WB was not outside with us now was that he was in his cubby wrapping Fortune's gift. He found out her birthday was tonight and we were going to surprise her with a party. Pickles was with him helping. WB stole Fortune a new wig and we were able to scrape up some money to buy a pack of Hostess cupcakes and candles for the center. He wanted it to be nice because nobody could find her dog *Leave Me Alone* all night, and she was in and out of sadness about it. It's amazing, at first she didn't want the dog and now she couldn't live without him.

"If you not talking about Fortune who you talking about?" I asked, trying to act uninterested in the only person who has kept my attention for the last few weeks.

"I'm talking about Everest. Be real with me if you not with nobody else."

"Man, I'm not thinking about that girl," I lied trying to look at everything except her pretty face. "First off, she not my type. Second of all I don't have no time to be liking nobody these days. The only thing on my mind right now is getting this murder beef off my back and staying out of jail. Who gives a fuck about anything else?"

"I do," he said looking at Gage. "I would give anything for it. Love that is."

I knew he was attracted to her, but this was the first time I saw it in his eyes. "Spirit, how come you never just go at her? If you want it go get it, man, before somebody else do."

"She's not interested," he said in a low voice. "I wish she was though. Because I would never hurt her feelings and I would give my life for her." He looked at me. "You know?"

"So you never told her you liked her?"

"Whenever I tried to go at her in a soft way, she manages to bring up how happy she is to have a friend like me in her life. She put me in the friend zone, Mad, and I can't get out of it."

"Maybe you should stop beating around the bush and go straight at her, man. The way you doing it is making you look soft. Walk up to her and say, I want to do right by you. Are you gonna let me or not? You act like you not a catch, Spirit. You practically run The Catacombs. If you wasn't down here running shit it would be total chaos. You have power and women love that. Look at all of the other chicks who go at you."

"But what if I go at her and she shoot me down?"

"Then at least you'll know you tried, Spirit."

"But I know she's in love with you," he said looking at me closely. I guess he was trying to pick me apart to see where my mind was.

"Listen, I like Gage. As a matter of fact I care about her a lot. But it's no different than how I feel about all of ya'll. I got so much going on right now that I can't be in a relationship anyway. And even if I did have time it wouldn't be with her. Trust me, you safe as far as I'm concerned." I looked at Gage. "That's all you, young."

When I said that WB walked out with seven cupcakes sitting on a piece of cardboard box. A candle sat in the middle of each of them and the glow lit up his chocolate face.

"Happy birthday, baby," he said walking up to Fortune.

I'm not going to lie; the look on Fortune's face had me feeling some kind of way. She's good people and it's about time one of the good guys got what they wanted for a change.

"Happy Birthday to you, happy birthday to you, happy birthday dear Fortune, happy birthday to you," Everyone sang and they were even able to get a note or two out of me.

When we were done Fortune wiped the tears out her eyes and went to hug WB. WB welcomed the embrace but not before pushing more hair into her face to cover it. It was a lot to look at her full mug.

After Fortune took off the old wig and put on the new one, WB reached into his back pocket and handed her some fake diamond earrings. I didn't know he had those.

"Oh my, God," she cried putting the earrings on. "They are prettier than the ones my dog ate. She got sad again but we cheered her up. I wish we knew where the dog was.

Fortune floated around The Pit swinging her hair from left to right while the fake diamonds sparkled in her ears. I was feeling good until I looked behind WB and noticed something was off.

"Hey, man, where's Pickles?" I could feel my heart kicking at the walls of my chest. "I thought he was with you."

"What you talking about? He said he wanted to read you a story so I let him—"

"You let him what?" I pushed his chest, and the cupcakes fell out of his hands and to the ground. "Walk into The Catacombs by himself?" I pointed into his face. "I asked you not to take your eyes off of him when you said it was okay for him to come with you, and help with Fortune's gift. And you said you had it. So where is my little man?"

"I'm sorry, man, I—"

"Fuck sorry, that's why I can never trust you mothafuckas. Always telling me you got my back when you don't." I walked away from him.

I felt like committing murder.

"Where you going?" WB asked.

"To go find my son," I said.

"Your son?" I heard WB say as I disappeared into The Catacombs. "But he's not your kid."

⬤━━━━━━━━━━━━━━━━━━━━━━━━━━━━━⬤

After I spent two hours looking for Pickles in The Catacombs I still couldn't find him. I had a flashlight in one hand and a pan in the other. It wasn't until I heard soft whimpering down the South Wing where the shit pots were that I breathed a sigh of relief.

"Pickles, is that you?" I asked flashing the lights down the South Wing. The smell was sickening but I didn't care.

The whimpering was louder as I walked deeper into the darkness, but I couldn't hear any words. When I finally got to the area that he was in I almost couldn't hold the contents of my stomach. I shined the flashlight into the area and there Pickles was, in a dog cage with gray duct taped on his mouth and wrists.

"What the fuck?" I dropped the flashlight and the pan to open the cage. Once I had him in my arms I snatched the tape off of his mouth and hands.

"Thank you," he said shivering. "T-they, took me."

"Who took you, Pickles? You gotta kick shit real with me now because this is serious."

"I see you found him," someone said.

When I saw it was Pop Kill and Wicked, I jumped up, grabbed the flashlight and the pan. I pushed Pickles behind me and banged the pan against the walls. I scraped it from left to right, knowing that the sound would ring throughout The Catacombs and everybody would hear it. This was a known way to send a distress signal because the sound could be heard over everything, even the radio that we rocked sometimes at The Pit.

As people started coming into the area we were in, Pop killed looked at me and said, "Smart, very smart." He tucked something in the back of his shirt and I knew it was a weapon. "Because it was going to be your final night." He looked down at Pickles. "Both of you."

We were surrounded by a lot of people now.

After we had our barbeque, the West Wingers threw a barbeque celebration that we weren't invited too. The meaty odor of something cooking on the grill caused my stomach to rumble. But unlike when we had some extra food, Wicked and his crew didn't share with us. Even if they did I wasn't in the mood. I was too busy trying to put Pickles to sleep after what happened.

After two hours of rubbing his head, he finally dosed off until WB rushed frantically into my room.

"What is it?" I asked.

"You didn't hear, man?

"Hear what?"

"Fortune's real fucked up. Them West Wingers took shit too far now. They killed *Leave Me Alone* and…and…"

"And what?"

WB held onto his stomach and said, "They ate him. They fucking put him on the grill and ate him." He threw up in my doorway.

CHAPTER 21
MAD

After the shit they tried to do to Pickles and what happened to *Leave Me Alone*, Pickles stayed with me like vinegar to a cucumber. I would wake up in the morning, way before he did, and stay up until he went to sleep at night. He was a sleepwalker so I wanted to be sure he didn't go off and leave me. Since I had to go out and scramble up some money, Everest would help me keep an eye on him. She was as fucked up as I was about what Wicked and Pop Kill tried to do to us so I appreciated her help.

"He's sleep," Everest said sitting next to me on the bed. "Are you okay? I know that tossed your head around about what happened down the South Wing."

I shrugged. "I'm gonna to always be alright but I gotta think of something. Shit is getting out of hand down here."

I looked over at the small loveseat that Mad MaXXX helped me move into my cubby. Pickles looked peaceful, like nothing bothered him in the world. I wondered how he managed to be so strong despite people trying to get at him just to hurt me.

"You're good to him," she said, her voice sounded like notes from a piano.

"You say that shit all the time. I wish you'd stop."

"That's because I'm serious. He's lucky to have you."

I stood up. She was too nice sometimes and I needed to get away from her. "I'm sorry, Mad." She looked down at her hands and then up at me. "I have to keep reminding myself that you aren't mine."

"I'm nobody's."

She smiled. It was a half smile that only rose up on one side. "I know." She looked over at Pickles. "So what is your plan? I know you can't live up top right now because of everything that's going on up there too."

I sighed and sat next to her again. "For now I'm gonna keep an eye on him while we're down here. But I do gotta bounce soon. If I don't leave either I'm going to hurt Wicked or I'm going to kill him. Or I'll hurt him first and then kill him. At this point there's nothing else in the cards for me but death."

"He wasn't always that way. As a matter of fact when I came back I was surprised at how different he was. How hateful he was. I don't recognize him anymore."

"What happened?"

"Before you moved down here he was in control of everybody. He was the one who everyone went to if they needed something, despite Daze being the father figure. It was back in the day when he was with Gage and I guess when you came along he felt threatened."

"But I never said shit to this dude out the way before. I never wanted Gage either. And as far as running shit, that's the last thing on my mind. All I want to do is stay out of jail."

"You don't have to do anything to him. Before you came to The Catacombs, Gage and everybody else took his shit. But since you got here people started acting differently. It was like a cult before you got here and now people are realizing they can exist without him. Without submitting to his rules."

"Whatever change you talking about them making was on them not me."

"It's not wrong that people are changing, Mad. It's just fact. You did that for a lot of people and they look up to you for that. You need to be proud of it."

I decided to offer her a drink so that she would stop all the mind talk. Besides it was driving me crazy.

When the drinks were poured we spent the rest of the night talking about life down here and what we missed about the real world. I started to realize she wasn't the *bitch* I thought she was. She was a cool person who was just different. Just like me.

After some days she moved into my cubby to help me out with Pickles. At first I didn't know how I would feel about it. But before long I started to like her around and that scared me.

━━━━━━━━━━━━━━━━━━━━━━━━━━━━━

I was wide awoke after having another dream. It was of my mother again. I knew at that moment I had to tell somebody because it was driving me crazy. Why would she come to me in a dream since she didn't do shit for me in life?

This dream was just as weird. I was standing in front of a mirror, and my mother was brushing my face with the back of her hand. Every time she touched me instead of being repulsed I felt high. Like I was floating. When I was so high I could barely open my eyes she kissed me on the face and I woke up.

While Pickles and Everest were sleep I decided to go see Old Man Young about the nightmares, I wanted answers. When I walked into his cubby I was surprised to see him up already. It was like he was waiting on me.

I stood in his doorway and pulled my cap down. "Can I ask you a question?"

Normally he charged me a bottle of beer or something, but I was hoping he would answer my question for free this time. Every bit of the money I had now I saved up to make sure Pickles had something to eat.

"You got me a beer?" he asked as he adjusted his eye patch.

"Naw."

He looked me over. "I guess one question won't hurt. What is it?"

I walked inside of his cubby and looked down at him. I almost wanted to say never mind because there was nothing to prove that he could actually help me. "I've been having bad dreams a lot lately about my mother. We didn't have a relationship so it's strange."

"What was your dream about?"

I told him about the three dreams I had. When I was done he smiled. "You can't see what she's saying? It's as clear as the nose on your face. If your heart was open you wouldn't need my help."

I hated when people spoke in circles. "Listen, man, if I knew what she was trying to tell me I wouldn't be here. Now are you gonna answer my question or not?

He grabbed a piece of paper and a pen. "In your first dream you said your mother was cooking on the stove. On the stove was a pan"— he wrote down something— "You mentioned that a lizard was on the counter"— he wrote down something— "you said that on the table in front of you were eggs"— again he wrote down something— "you also said there was an apple on the stove, and that syrup was everywhere in front of you." When he was done he handed me the paper.

"I don't know what this means."

His eyebrows rose. "You can't read can you?"

Silence.

He snatched it away. "It doesn't matter I'll explain it to you. The *p* for the *pan*, along with the *l* for the *lizard*, the *e* for the *eggs*, the *a* for the *apple*, the *s* for the *syrup*, along with the *e* for the syrup being *everywhere* spells PLEASE."

"What does that mean?"

He frowned and seemed frustrated. "I'm not done quite yet, young man."

"My bad."

"The second dream you said had a *Frog, Owl, Rocks, Grapes, Ice, Valentine*, and a young lady who kept chanting *Ever*. If you take the first letter of each of those items you have the word *FORGIVE*."

My stomach felt jittery and I wanted to throw up.

"In your final dream you were sitting in front of a mirror. You also said you were—"

"High," I blurted out. "And as far as I know MH don't spell nothing."

"I see you know something about words after all," he frowned.

"I can spell *me*," I said proudly.

"I don't doubt that, but what you failed to realize is that words often have different meanings. So if you replace the *high* feeling you felt when your mother touched you, and called it *euphoria* instead you would have the letter *e*. Together they spell *me*. What your mother was asking was PLEASE FORGIVE ME." He looked at me. "Does that make any sense to you?"

I stumbled backwards. My mother never apologized for shit. She was a selfish bitch until the day she died and I wasn't trying to hear shit he was saying. He didn't know the whore, but I did. *Personally*. I knew it was a mistake to come here. What would make me think that he could tell me anything about life when he was living in the slums too?

"Mad, I don't know what kind of relationship you had with your mother, but it sounds to me like she's asking for your forgiveness. So that her soul can rest. Maybe you should give it to her."

"Fuck my mother and fuck her soul! If I have anything to do with it she will rot in hell forever."

⸻

After I left Old Man Young's spot I went back to my cubby. When I made sure that both Pickles and Everest were okay and still sleeping, I decided to go to The Pit. The moment I walked outside, I was angry when I saw Fierce sitting on the ground next to the trashcan sleep. I guess he burned so many bridges here that nobody wanted him to live in their cub.

I was about to turn around thinking he would try to talk to me when Spirit walked out to The Pit. "What the fuck is he doing here?" he asked me. "I haven't seen him in weeks."

"Sleep I guess," I responded. "Why, you beefing with him too?"

Spirit looked down at him. It looked as if he felt bad for him. "I just don't trust him anymore. He stole something from me and I never forgave him for that shit."

I looked at him. Damn, nobody was safe from his thievery. "That's your man not mine."

"Well I'm about to wake the nigga up." Spirit walked over to him and pushed him hard. "Get the fuck up, Fierce. You not supposed to be here anyway! You were voted out."

"You trying to wake him up or shake him to death?"

Spirit ignored me. He was pushing him so hard that I thought Fierce's neck would snap. "Get the fuck up!"

"Just leave the nigga alone," I said about to walk back inside to go to my cubby. "He's probably high."

Spirit dropped to his knees and put his fingers on his throat. All of a sudden the look on his face changed from anger to sadness. He scooted backwards on the ground and stopped next to my foot.

"What's wrong?" I asked looking down at him.

"He's dead."

I heard him but I couldn't understand what he was *really* saying. "What you mean he's dead." I looked over at him. If anything he looked sleep.

In a lower whisper he said, "He's dead. He's gone."

While I was looking at him, Wicked, Pop Kill and some more West Wingers walked outside. "Fuck is up with Fierce?" Wicked asked looking down at him.

Spirit stood up and said, "He's dead."

Before that moment I didn't think Wicked had a heart. But as sure as my name is Madjesty, the dude dropped down on the ground and immediately started performing CPR on Fierce. It was useless though. Because I could already tell he was dead. His body appeared stiff.

Ten minutes later everybody seemed to come out into The Pit. A lot of people were crying after they learned that Fierce was dead and I felt fucked up for how I treated him. That's until I realized he had to do this shit to himself. Why did he have to go get himself killed? This is the last thing I needed right now.

Pickles walked up to me, grabbed my hand and started crying too. Although Pickles knew Fierce I think he was really crying because everyone else was.

Later on that night we buried him across from The Pit. In the place we kept most of our dead. Spirit said a few words in his honor and when we were done I was exhausted. Mainly because Pickles wouldn't stop crying. Gage kept rubbing her temples. It was one thing to lose just another person from The Catacombs, but it was another thing to lose someone you broke bread with everyday.

We were at The Pit looking at the fire when Wicked said to me, "You know it's all your fault right?"

"My fault?" It was so ridiculous I almost laughed. "How is this my fault?"

"Because he told me you wouldn't talk to him even though he begged you. Told me he wanted to apologize but you didn't hear him out. What's up with that? We may have had our problems but Fierce was a good friend and now he's gone."

"Nigga, I don't owe you shit, especially not an explanation. You betta be glad you still got your face after what you did to Pickles. Stay the fuck away from me. I'm warning you." I grabbed Pickles' hand and stepped off.

CHAPTER 22

MAD

It was *Tell All Tuesday* again and I was at The Pit with Spirit, Gage, WB, Everest and Pickles. Although I could tell that most of us were still thinking about Fierce. We needed to take our minds off the fact that he was gone.

I didn't let them know that I was taking his death hard. As much as I hated Wicked he was right. Fierce had done everything in his power to connect with me and I knocked him down. Now it was too late. Too late to tell him it wasn't that deep. Who the fuck am I to point a finger in someone's face after everything I'd been through? I let him down. While I was thinking about Fierce, Motor Angel was *Turning Tell All*. When she finished I knew it would be the last time we saw her too. I was looking at her like it would be the last time I saw her.

"Anybody else want to turn Tell All?" Spirit asked.

When I saw Everest raise her hand my heart thumped. "I'd like to go next please."

"No you won't," I yelled not realizing it was so loud until I looked at everyone's faces. "Just sit down and let somebody else talk for a change. It ain't always about you, Everest."

"It's okay, Mad," she smiled looking into my eyes. "I really want to."

"Everest, I'm begging you not to talk about your past. Just leave it alone." I didn't want her doing that shit. I was just getting to know her and I wanted her to stay around. What I couldn't say out loud was that I needed her, and Pickles did too.

"If she wants to talk let her," Wicked said entering The Pit with Pop Kill. "Its high time people started letting you know that you aren't running shit around here."

"You don't know what you talking about." I told him. "You always flapping your lips but you never saying shit."

I focused back on Everest. I know she wasn't my girl but I didn't want her to *Turn Tell All* tonight only to leave in the morning. It was mainly for Pickles because he had gotten use to her being around. At least that's what I was telling myself.

I felt like I wanted to snatch her out of here. Convince her that she didn't need to give her story to anybody but it was too late she was talking. Why is she doing this shit to me? And why can't I tell her how I feel?

When she looked down into the fire I knew it was over.

"I've lied to most of you," she said softly. "Well, I've lied to all of you." The glow from the flames turned her eyes into caramel candies.

I didn't want her to do this.

I didn't want her to do this!

"Every time I leave here I never go on any crazy adventure. I don't travel the world or hang out with famous movie stars either. When I leave it's not because I want adventure. It's because I'm scared. Scared of getting too close to you all. Scared of getting to know you all because I'm not sure how long you will continue to love me." Tears rolled down her face, and she wiped them away. "I'm not who I say I am."

"Everest, it's okay," Gage said.

"No it's not," she said wiping her eyes. "I'm a fraud, a fake, and I don't deserve your love. And losing Fierce reminds me how much of a liar I am."

"That's not true, Everest," Gage said approaching her. "I saw the passport and everything, from when you got the stamps. You've been everywhere. To China, Rome and—"

"I haven't been anywhere and the stamps are all fake," she yelled cutting her off. "Unless you consider a train ride to New York or Philly some place," she continued wiping her eyes again. "I wanted everybody to think I was somebody. I wanted everybody to think that even though I stayed here, in the tunnel, I didn't have to be here. I wanted you to believe that I was here visiting and not staying because unlike you I had some place else to go."

"But...you always had money," Gage said softly. "How?"

"I would sell my body before I came back." She looked at me. "I didn't care about myself or anybody else until now. I'm a failure."

It was now completely silent. She was a whore. Just like my mother and I still loved her.

Later that night when we were in my cubby she didn't say anything. When I heard her crying I wanted to go to her but I was mad. Pickles even tried to read one of his favorite stories but she acted like he was bothering her.

The next morning, something told me it would be a bad day. And when I turned around in the cubby I was right.

Everest was gone.

The day after Everest left, Old Man Young said I caught the flu because I was lovesick. Not sure how one catches the flu because of being in love but I do know I was fucked up in the head. My temperature was high and I was sweating.

Spirit, Gage, WB and Pickles stood in my cubby looking down at me like I was going to die. I could tell by the look in their eyes that they were worried.

"I'm fine," I told them feeling worse every time I opened my mouth. "I just need to hang back and relax that's all."

"You're not fine," Spirit said firmly. "You sick, man. And the air down here can't make things much better. You may have to go to a hospital. Real talk!"

"You already know that's not happening," I responded. "I'm not trying to go to jail just to get over no cold."

"I'm sorry she left you," Gage said, "If you chose me I would've never left you."

"Why would you say something like that to him right now?" WB asked."I just wanted Mad to know that it was a sucker move on Everest's part. I am grown you know? I do get to speak my mind."

"What Everest did is her business and I don't give a fuck," I said as every muscle on my body shivered. "Ya'll act like we were in a relationship or something. And if ya'll came in here to rap my head off about that chick, you can kick concrete."

"We not coming in here for that," Spirit said. He walked into the doorway and told somebody to come inside. "We came to bring Old Man Young to check you out."

Although I was annoyed maybe he could give me something for a broken heart, body and mind. Like he did when I had the urinary thing.

He stepped closer to me with his dirty eye patch. "Well you definitely have the flu," he said after checking me for an hour. He looked over at Spirit. "Go get her a box of tea, lemon, and some Hennessy. Feed it to her every hour on the hour. After that both her broken heart and body should be fine."

I hated that he mentioned my heart because it made me feel soft. Instead of arguing with him I went to sleep. When I woke up I felt something on my ankle. When I looked down I saw Pickles at the foot of my bed. He was massaging my feet for some reason. Not sure what his purpose was but it felt good and I drifted back to sleep.

When I woke up about an hour later I smelled tea and Hennessy. Spirit handed me a white Styrofoam cup and I took my first sip. It was warm and I downed it all before handing it back to him hoping that he'd give me some more. For some reason I felt worse. It was as if the tunnel was spinning.

"Mad, you okay?" Spirit asked me.

I knew what was happening. I was dying. So I looked up at him, Gage, WB and Pickles. In the drunk zone I said, "I just wanted ya'll to know that I fuck with you. *Hard.* I might not always say it but it's true."

"Mad, chill out," WB said. "You tripping right now."

"I'm not tripping. I'm being real, and I need ya'll to look after my man Pickles." I swallowed and chills covered my body. "I don't think I'm going to make it. I don't think…"

I drifted off into a deep sleep and started dreaming. In my dream I was standing in front of Mr. Nice Guy, the only man other than my father who cared about me. We were in a park with real big green trees all around us. The trees had red fruit that looked like large strawberries the size of apples.

"How are you, Madjesty?" He asked smiling down at me. "How are you really?"

"I'm fine," I swallowed looking around. The place felt crazy. "Am I dead?"

"Not yet," he smiled. "I just wanted to tell you that your mother is here with me and she's fine. A lot has changed since she passed over and she wanted me to ask you to please forgive her."

I was immediately angry. "Why would I forgive her?" I frowned. "And why would you ask me to? It's because of her that you're dead. You should be on my side."

"Your mother was sick in the mind, Madjesty. She didn't know how to be a good mother because she didn't have a mother to show her the way. But more importantly I'm asking you to forgive her because if you do you'll be better for it. Physically and mentally. I promise you."

"And how do you know? You left me too," I yelled beating on my chest. "You fucking left me in the world by myself after you made me love you. All for a woman who didn't like you and got you killed. My precious mother that you keep talking about."

"I know that's how it looks and I'm so sorry about that Madjesty. But you must understand that I love you and I always will. The thing is, your mother loves you too and she is sorry for everything she did to you and your sister. She wants you to get your son and repair the bond with Jayden. People make mistakes and so did she."

"You don't know shit about my mother! She ain't nothing but a lying bitch, even in death. And I will never, ever forgive her for what she put me through."

He sighed. "I can tell you're still in pain but give it some thought, kiddo," he said. "I promise it will be worth your while. And now you have to wake up because I have a special gift waiting for you."

When I opened my eyes Everest was at my door.

CHAPTER 23

MAD

I was sitting on the bed in my cubby and Everest was behind me brushing my hair while Pickles read me a story. Although I didn't have the flu anymore. I wasn't feeling myself yet.

"How you feeling?" Everest asked. "You seem distant."

I looked over at Pickles who kept flipping the pages of his book. "I'm fine. Sometimes I feel weak but other than that I'm good."

"I meant how do you feel about me?"

"I don't know what you want me to say, Everest."

"Do you care about me? Since I've been back you've been keeping your distance and I kind of want to hear how you feel out of your mouth. Not from other people."

I sighed. "I don't know what I'm feeling. I think it's too early to go there."

She stopped brushing my hair. "I don't want to fall in love with you for no reason. If this thing is real between us then I wanna know now. I need to hear you say it, Mad."

Instead of giving her what she wanted I don't talk. I feel like if I admit that I got feelings for her things will change again and she'll end up leaving me like everyone else I cared about in my life.

I guess my quietness irritated her because she jumped up and walked toward the door.

Before she walked out I said, "I care about you, I just need you to give me time to think things through. Every relationship I've ever been in failed. I like to take things slow. Either you get with that or you can do us both a favor and bounce now."

●━━━━━━━━━━━━━━━━━━━━━━━━●

Pickles was with me in the soup kitchen. I couldn't keep my eyes off of him for some reason today. I imagined that my son Cassius looked just like him and that he knew how much I loved him even though I never got a chance to tell him.

I was watching him eat bread when Father Brian walked over to us.

"Hello, Madjesty," he said.

It was then that I remembered he said my full name before when I was beating the brakes off of the nigga in front of the kitchen.

"How did you know my first name?"

"I saw it on the Wanted Poster."

I swallowed.

"Don't worry though, you're safe here," he smiled.

I'm starting to feel a creepy vibe about him. It may be because he's so nice, and I can't find another reason why he would help me.

"This young man seems hungry," he sat next to me and looked over at Pickles. "Hey little—"

"Don't touch him," I said catching him before he placed his hand on his hair. "He's not like that."

"Like what?"

"You know…gay."

He frowned. "Mad, I know many priests in my religion have developed a bad reputation, but I will assure you that I'm not one of them. Anyway I'm coming over here to talk to you."

"About what?" I stirred the soup in my bowl.

"About what happened when you were last here, with the teenager out front."

I dropped the spoon. "I thought you said you weren't going to snitch. So what you a liar now?"

"Mad," he said calmly, "please listen to me. What happened that day was unfortunate and I understood why your anger was directed toward him. But what I wanted to talk about was what you said when you were beating him."

I frowned. "What you talking about?"

He leaned back into his seat and looked at me as if I were confused. "You don't remember?"

"What you talking about?" I repeated even more frustrated. "If I remembered I would say so. Plus I probably say a lot of shit when I'm angry."

"You kept saying the name Jayden, and you mentioned how you hated her. Who is she?"

I was sitting in my cubby thinking about what Father Brian said. I don't remember calling Jayden's name or saying that I hated her. But I'm not surprised. My sister stabbed me in my back when she took side of outsiders instead of mine.

I was trying to get my mind right but I smelled them before he even got to my cubby. Just like most West Wingers, he stank of dirt and grime. Blazer stood in my doorway, and I cracked an empty bottle to use it as a weapon.

"Fuck you doing in my room, snitch?"

"I came to talk," he said eyeing the weapon. "I'm not coming to cause no problems or nothing so you can ease up some."

"Fuck do you wanna talk about then?" I'm gripping the glass in my hand so hard I can feel it starting to crack again.

"There is a plan going down next week that involves you," Blazer warned. "And all I'm doing is coming to let you know about it so that you can prepare."

My heartbeat rocked. "By who?"

"Who do you think? Wicked and Pop Kill."

"Why you telling me this?"

"Because you didn't tell anybody about how I left you hanging at the grocery store, and this is my way of paying you back," he paused.

"But after this my debt to you is over."

CHAPTER 24
MAD

"Gage, why you coming at me sideways again?" I asked as I sat in my cubby on the bed. "We been through this. I'm not feeling you."

She was blowing me because the plan was to walk Everest and Pickles to the entrance of The Catacombs later so we could grab something to eat up top. But thanks to this argument, I couldn't go anywhere. Why won't she just get over me? It seemed like women wanted you more when you didn't want them.

"I feel like you want me to lie to you, and that's fucked up, Gage, because you putting me in a fucked up position."

"I'm not saying I want you to lie to me. I just want to know why you didn't want to fuck with me, but you got up with my friend instead. I mean, what's so special about Everest?"

"It ain't about her being special. It's about us having a connection that you and I don't have."

"So you are admitting to being in love with her."

"I got feelings for her, Gage. That's all I know for sure."

"You so fucking stupid," she said. "She got you wide open even after she said she's not who she claims to be. If anything you need to be running the other way."

"Who in The Catacombs is who they claim to be?" I looked into her eyes. "Name one person, Gage. Who down here ain't running from a past? Or lying?"

"You know what I mean, Mad."

"All I know is this, I fuck with you, and hard too, but I will never like you the way that you want me to like you. Ever. Plus I'm bad news, Gage. How come you never gave Spirit a chance?"

"Spirit?" she laughed. "What the fuck are you talking about?"

"I'm talking about the fact that Spirit wants to be with you, but you don't give him the time of day." I know it was wrong to throw my man under the bus but I hoped it would work to my advantage...and his.

"He told you that?"

"Yes."

"I don't know about all that but I do know this," she said. "One day you're going to realize you made a mistake about fucking with Everest over me and when that happens don't say shit to me because I won't be here for you."

"Aye, Mad," Spirit screamed in the hallway.

I pushed past Gage to meet him outside of my cubby. "What's wrong?" I asked feeling like something was way off. "Pickles okay?"

Spirit leaned on his knees. He was out of breath. "Some...somebody was just here asking for you by name at the entrance. So don't leave The Catacombs."

"What they say?"

"They wouldn't give me any information. It was two white men."

"Were they cops?"

"I'm not sure," he said standing up. "But they looked pretty official to me."

"I got to get out of here, man," I said walking back into my cubby. "It's just a matter of time before they come down here."

"Mad, you can't leave The Catacombs," Spirit said following me inside. Gage was right behind him. "Them mothafuckas ain't trying to come in here, trust me. If you go outside you going to be out in the open and they are liable to find you. Just chill here more and if we have to we will be on lookout twenty four seven."

As much as I hated to depend on other people I didn't have a choice at the moment. For the first time in a long time, my life depended on someone else and I hoped it wouldn't be a mistake.

I was in The Pit eating some hot dogs that we copped and put over the grill. Pickles was beside me and Everest was across from me. She been acting funny all night. Really she hadn't been right since I said I didn't want the relationship. I wanted to talk to her but every time I asked what was wrong she said nothing.

WB was fucking Fortune in The Dump and from where we stood we could hear their moans. I guess they're an item now.

I blocked their sounds out of my mind and was just about to ask Everest if she was cool again when Wicked and Pop Kill walked outside. Pickles walked closer to me and grabbed my hand. I guess he was scared.

East Wingers didn't fuck with Wicked anymore and didn't pay him any attention.

WB and Fortune finished their thing in The Dump and walked over to the crowd.

"What's up," Wicked said eying the hot dogs. Nobody said anything. "Wow, even after Fierce died we still can't get along. Ya'll still choosing that bitch over me."

"Just chill out," Gage said. "Why you always saying something stupid out your face? If we don't want to talk to you, go find somebody who does."

"Yeah, you need to relax, Wicked," Everest added. "Because I'm tired of hearing your fucking mouth too. Since I've been back all you do is be negative."

He walked up to her and I immediately blocked him. Pickles ran over to Fortune who picked him up.

"You drunk and you're tripping right now," I told him. "You need to chill the fuck out, Wicked. I'm done with how you been carrying people around here. The shit ends today. And by the way, if you planning to do anything to me you better suit up because I'm ready."

"Are you," he smirked. I could tell he was surprised that I found out about his plans for me.

"I am. You better back the fuck off."

"And if I don't stop what are you going to do? Huh?" He gritted his teeth.

"You have no idea do you? You really don't know the kind of person I can be because I bite my tongue so much. Don't you know that the quietest ones are the most deadly?"

He laughed and walked back over to Pop Kill who was smirking at me. "All I know is you killed Rose and because you refuse to leave, you got the cops coming down here fucking with us," he laughed. "You don't even take care of your own son. You trying to replace him with Pickles. You are disloyal to your own blood but you want to be loyal to us?"

I was so angry I could feel hot tears streaming down my face. "First off I never claimed loyalty to you. Second of all you don't know what the fuck you talking about when it comes to my life. Or my kid."

"Of course I do," he winked. "Do you or do you not have a child that you have abandoned?"

"Mad, you don't have to answer—"

"Shut the fuck up," I said cutting Everest off. I focused back on him. "My past is my business and if I do decide to reveal my business. It won't be when you in the room."

"It's just like I thought," he laughed. "You're a dead-beat mother."

CHAPTER 25

MAD

Earlier today I got word that Wicked was making it his personal business to find out *exactly* what the cops wanted with me. The fake ass reason he gave everybody in The Catacombs was that he wanted to protect them since it's obvious they couldn't protect themselves. So by talking to the cops he would find out what they wanted.

I wanted to kill this dude so badly I couldn't see straight. I started to do it too, until Spirit and WB pulled me backwards when we were in The Pit. Calling me a deadbeat rubbed me the wrong way. It made me feel like my mother.

I needed somebody to talk to so I decided to go see Old Man Young again.

"What can I help you with this time, Mad?" he asked as I walked into his room, holding a can of warm beer.

"I have to ask you something."

"Go ahead." He took the beer from me.

"I need to know...if I should...I mean go and see my—"

"Yes," he said popping the beer open.

I frowned. "Yes what?"

"Yes you should go and see about your son. It's time Mad, because until you can fully deal with your past you won't be able to move on in life."

"But what about my sister? She's taking care of him and she doesn't want me around. How can I convince her to change her mind?"

"I can't tell you how to do it but it's time for you to address the relationship you don't have with your family and move on. If you don't things will get worse here before they get better. I also know that you can't make up for not being a mother to your child by taking care of Pickles. You aren't supposed to be down here. You never were. You're a natural born leader, and its time you realize it."

"You don't understand, everybody here depends on me. I'm not only responsible for Pickles but what about Spirit, Gage and WB? They haven't been the same since Fierce died and if I leave right now that will fuck them up."

"Now are you talking about your friends and Pickles or Everest?"

"She's not the only person I'm thinking about but yeah, she needs me too."

I knew he couldn't understand and something told me that I was wasting my breath talking to him, but what I was saying was true. Jayden had Cassius, and Cassius had her but nobody needed me but my friends, Everest and Pickles.

"Mad, you have to live your life for you. Like I said you don't belong here."

"You know what, I shouldn'tve come here," I turned to walk out. "I'm gone."

I left his cubby but was still thinking about what he said to me. I wasn't making excuses. I just needed time before I made a move like reaching out to my sister, and I didn't care what he thought. This was my life and he had no clue about the things I've been through.

When I walked into my cubby, Pickles was sitting on the edge of the bed crying while clutching a piece of paper. I ran over to him, wondering what he was doing in here by himself. The last person watching him was Everest so where was she now?

"What's going on, Lil man?" I sat next to him. "Why you crying?"

He couldn't catch his breath so I took the piece of paper out of his hand. The moment I opened it my heart sank. Although I couldn't read every word on the page I understood three of them. *Sorry...leaving...bye.*

I can't believe it. She made me fall for her and then she left me.

Again.

I stayed in my room the entire day after Everest left. When I found the letter that Pickles was holding, I had Spirit read it by telling him that my eyes were bad. I didn't want him knowing I couldn't read.

"Aight, man, here goes," he said standing in front of me.

Dear Mad,

I battled with whether or not to write you this letter because I knew there was nothing anybody could say to stop me from leaving. But I love you and at the very least you deserve an explanation. I'm sorry, but I can't stay here anymore. It was so difficult trying to prevent myself from leaving early on. I know you don't believe me, but it's hard walking away from you and I miss you already.

I hope you understand my need to be alive and to experience life outside of The Catacombs. Give Pickles a hug and kiss for me. I love you and it's still okay for you not to say it because I know you don't love me back. Before I left I gave you an opportunity to tell me my observations were different and you didn't.

Goodbye.

Love Everest.

When Spirit was done he stood in front of me. "Damn, man, I'm sorry."

"Just leave," I whispered

"Mad, you shouldn't be—"

"Get the fuck out," I yelled.

When he left my first instinct was to rip my cubby up and destroy everything. But after awhile I realized that Everest did me a favor by bailing on me. Without her around I didn't have to worry about making sure she ate, or making sure she was comfortable in my spot. All I cared about was me and Pickles.

I was in my room trying to drink my troubles away, while Pickles read a story to me when I heard a bunch of moaning outside. I jumped up and moved toward the sound.

"Come with me, Pickles," I said. "I don't want you leaving my sight."

He walked behind me and I grabbed his hand. When I made it closer to the sound I noticed an East Winger named CEO Charles was pushing a huge electric stove down the aisle. Some bullshit was always happening down here. It was sitting on a wheeled wooden platform. The wheels rolling over the rocks sent screeching noises throughout the tunnel. Fuzzy Bear was behind him helping him push the stove.

"What ya'll doing with the stove?" Spirit asked stepping out of his hole.

"What it look like?" CEO Charles responded. "I'm taking the stove to my cubby so I can make some real food around here. Don't worry; it's electric and not gas. Nobody gonna die in they sleep."

"I don't care what it is," Spirit continued. "Where do you think you putting it? You know we don't have the electrical power to handle a stove. You gotta take it out of here."

"Oh yeah, well how come we got enough power to handle your fridge and hot plate but not my stove?" He asked Spirit.

"Because my shit is small and doesn't have that much wattage. That thing is huge." Spirit shot back.

"It'll be fine," CEO Charles responded. "If I gotta use it as a dresser instead, then so be it. Just relax."

"I don't want you bringing it in here," Spirit continued with an attitude. "If it's here I know you gonna use it so you gotta take it back."

"Look, it's my stove and I'm going to keep it," CEO Charles yelled. "But if you man enough to make me change my mind, step to me." When Spirit didn't respond he said, "That's what I thought."

Me and Spirit watched them push the stove into the cubby. Fifteen minutes later I could smell the meaty scent of bacon rushing through the tunnel. I started to think that the stove wasn't such a bad idea. Maybe I could make a complete hot meal on the stove too. But before I could take in another breath of the bacon fragrance the power went out.

"I knew that shit," Spirit said to me. I handed him my flashlight and he turned it on. "I fucking knew this would happen!" He pointed the light toward the entrance. "You see what the fuck I'm saying, CEO? I hope the shit was worth it!"

"Sorry, man," he responded into the darkness.

I reached for Pickles who was shivering and said, "It's cool, Lil man. We just gotta find E1 and E2 so they can turn the lights back on."

The three of us went through the tunnel searching for the engineers with flashlights. It didn't take us long to find E2, because he was dragging a metal ladder while holding a flashlight. The sound of the ladder scraping against the floor was deafening.

"Where's your father?" Spirit asked him. "We need him to put us back onto the electric tap."

"I'm not sure, but I can turn the power back on myself, trust me," he said out of breath. The flashlight Spirit shined on him showcased his sweaty face. "Don't worry." We all knew E2 did crack but he tried to hide it.

"I don't, E2," Spirit said. "If something happens to you up there it's going to be on my conscious. And I know your father would never forgive me."

E2 frowned, and for a second he looked like he wanted to hurt him. "You aight, man?" I asked. "'Cause you look like you want to get something off your shoulders."

E2 turned his attention from Spirit and onto me. "Naw, I'm good," he said softening his expression. "But I can really help you guys if you let me. Besides my father is nowhere to be found and I know the wires. Let me put the city back on, Spirit. He taught me everything he knows."

Spirit looked at him while he shined the light against his face. "Go ahead, man, and make it quick before these bugs and rats start taking over."

E2 acted like he hit the lottery. He dragged his ladder to the lamppost in The Crossroads and set it up. Me, Pickles and Spirit followed him. I watched with the light shining on his back how he did what he did. I wanted to know how to turn the lights on if they ever went off again.

E2 was right about his expertise. Five minutes later the electricity was restored. And when I turned around I was looking in my father's face.

CHAPTER 26
MAD

I was standing in The Pit with my jaw hanging. I couldn't believe I was looking at my father. Although I knew he was not scared of no one. I was still amazed how he was standing in The Catacombs like it was nothing and I admired him all over again.

A few people walked out into The Pit and gave me looks but nobody said anything. He wasn't supposed to be here, because he was an outsider and it was against our rules. But I think the fact that he walked into the tunnel to get me when other people would've turned and run away gave the residents respect for him. For the moment anyway.

As we stood over the fire I looked him over. Although his eyes looked tired he was still handsome and I was starting to see myself in him. I wondered would Cassius look the same way too. He was wearing a low haircut and a black leather strap crossed his chest, which held the hatchet he took everywhere on his back. On his face was a pair of black-rimmed glasses. I guess his vision was leaving because he didn't wear them before.

"You know I've been worried sick about you right?" he asked me. "Madjesty, what you doing?"

I looked down at my shoes. In the beginning my father never expressed any type of emotion toward me. As a matter of fact he denied me to my mother and his friends. Our relationship was so crazy that the simplest way to explain it was this. My mother fucked my father and my sister's father at the same time. And because she was ovulating, both of their sperm hit her egg and she had one baby by my father, and one baby by Jayden's father. So that even though we twins, we have different fathers.

When I originally told my father that I was his daughter, he denied me. Soon afterwards we got into a few life and death scenarios together and I knew he loved me based on his actions. He wanted to protect me and at first it was hard to take. But even then he never really showed it until now.

"I'm not doing nothing, pops," I said. "But where have you been?" I asked skipping the subject.

"Outside of worrying about where my son was, I been on the run again. I ganked these niggas who were running this drug house out DC. Some kind of way they found out I was involved and now they looking for me. Any other time you know I'd stay around and deal with it, but I haven't had an army behind me for months. I'm solo in these streets right now, Madjesty. So I'm going to get away, get my money together and take care of them niggas later."

I frowned. "If you can get away how come you just won't stay gone? Especially if you say you got people looking for you. Why come back?"

"Cause that's not me."

I focused on my Hennessey bottle. "But what if you come back and they kill you? Will it be worth it then?"

"Why would you even say something like that? I'm Teflon, Madjesty. And ain't nobody gonna take me out of this world unless I'm ready." And then, as if he suddenly realized where we were he said, "But you never answered my question. What you doing here?"

"What you mean?"

"This place not for you," he said looking around. "If I didn't see your sneakers, I wouldn't know you were my son." He grabbed my curly ponytail. "Why you playing yourself like this, Mad? You better than this. You better than these people."

"I didn't know I was playing myself."

"Well you are. You might not have had the best when you were growing up, but you got family now. You got me and you know that." I looked away from him. "You do know that don't you?"

"Yes," I nodded. "I know."

"I was getting ready to say," he chuckled. "I'm in a tunnel talking to you over a trash can fire. Give me some credit when I say I'm in your corner."

"I know you are," I laughed.

"Good, so when you gonna get out of here and get your son back? I don't know if you realize it or not, but that sister of yours is carrying on like Cassius is her kid. I need you to correct that."

Just the thought of her pretending to be his mother made me hot. "I can't take care of him—"

"So you gonna be a deadbeat?" he interrupted. "Like your whore ass mother was before she died?"

"I would get Cassius if I could—"

"Do you want your son back or not?" he asked strongly.

"I…'cause…."

"Madjesty, do you want him back? Because if you do I can take you to go get him tonight and there would be nothing nobody could do to stop me...to stop us."

"Pops, it's not that simple. I mean, where we gonna go if I get him? Here?"

"No. You, me and my grandson could go to Texas and start all over. Antoinette has some property down there and she knows I want my family together." He grabbed my hand. "Come with me, Mad and let's go get your son. Because I'm going to tell you what I know to be truth, she cannot be trusted."

My heart thumped inside of my chest. I wanted my son, I know I did, but what if I couldn't take care of him? What if he doesn't recognize me? What if he cries when I hold him? What if Jayden doesn't let me have him? What if I'm a bad mother, like my mother? What if I...what if...I...beat my child too, like my mother beat me?

"You a good person, Madjesty," my father said to me as if he could hear my thoughts. "You nothing like your father, or mother, and you will never abuse Cassius. I know it. You're better than me, and your mother." He looked sad. "Let's go get him."

"I can't go with you, Pops. Not right now anyway."

He exhaled hard. Like he had been holding his breath for a while.

Trying to change the subject I said, "How did you know I was here anyway?"

"I found a piece of paper in the car the other day that dropped out of Antoinette's purse while she was cleaning it. It had your name on it, with this location. I'm not going to lie, I was going to kill her when I found out she knew where you were and didn't tell me, because she knows how hard I been looking for you. I let it go because at least you are still alive." He paused again. "Look, if you not coming with me how long are you going to stay here?"

"Not too much longer." I looked around. "I got myself into some shit that's making it hard to stay."

"Well how can I get in contact with you if you're here? I'm talking about phone calls."

I gave him Father Brian's information at the soup kitchen. He didn't write anything down but I know he held the information tightly it in his memory.

"I don't know if I ever told you this before," he said to me, "but I…I…lo…love you," he stuttered.

My eyes widened. "You love me?"

"Yes, you're my son, Madjesty. And I hate that you gotta do whatever you gotta do here. But I also understand that this is your journey. Not mine. I didn't start growing up until I found out you were actually my kid. But you need to also know that you're not like the rest of these mothafuckas here. You're loved, kiddo. I might not be the best father, but I'm still *your* father. We all we got."

"I understand," I said trying to hold back my own tears.

He took off my cap and wrestled up my hair before slapping my cap back on. The moment I pushed my hat over my eyes, Wicked walked into The Pit. "They said it was true but I was like naw, she's not crazy enough to have an outsider in The Catacombs. When she knows the rules," Wicked said. "I guess I'm wrong."

"I know the rules but this my father. Don't worry he's about bounce in a minute anyway."

"I don't give a fuck about what he's going to do in the future," he said as if my pops wasn't standing there. "You know the rules and the rules are no outsiders unless it's put to a vote. Was there a vote that I didn't know about? Because I'm confused."

I know my father is vicious but I didn't know he was quick too. Because before I could say anything, he grabbed Wicked by the neck and choked him.

CHAPTER 27

MAD

My armpits were dripping in sweat. I didn't see this shit coming. I was standing in front of Old Man Young, The Parable and one other elder as they prepared to judge my fate. To Old Man Young's right was Wicked and he wore a huge grin on his face. After all the shit he'd done he finally got what he wanted. The possibility of me being thrown out.

Behind me were my friends, Spirit, WB and Gage. I knew this wouldn't end well so I was glad they were there.

"Mad, you are being brought here because of what happened yesterday in The Pit. Do you understand?"

Yesterday when my pops choked Wicked out, me, Spirit and Gage was able to pull Wicked into his cubby without being seen by anybody else. To make it seem that Wicked was drunk and that my father hadn't done anything to him, we put the last of my Hennessey in his hand and splashed it all over his clothes. We did all we could to set up the scene. It was a dumb idea and our plan failed.

First it looked good because Wicked didn't wake up any that night. I was alone in my cubby talking to Pickles hoping that shit would be okay. But in the morning Spirit walked in with Gage and they had serious expressions on their faces. I knew what was up. Wicked not only remembered but he also snitched. I was mad at myself for not letting my father kill him and dump his body out back. Instead I spared his life and this is how he repaid me.

It took everything in my power to convince my pops to leave The Catacombs. He didn't go until I promised him that I was going to be okay.

"I understand that this is some bullshit," I said to Old Man Young. "Everybody here knows that Wicked was fucking with me and he finally got what he deserved. Choked out."

Spirit put his hand on my shoulder and whispered, "Mad, please don't give them all of that. We don't want you to leave."

"I don't give a fuck," I told him. I focused back on Old Man Young and the others. "I have eaten this mothafuckas shit for too long, and he got what he was due. He tried to kill me several times and he even tried to take out my little man." I looked over at Pickles who was with Fortune. "I'm glad the shit happened and I should've let him kill him."

"So you're saying that you aren't apologetic?" Old Man Young said.

"I'm saying fuck this nigga," I said looking into his eyes. "And I'm saying fuck everybody else who has a problem with it."

Old Man Young sighed. "Well, I guess I'll have to talk it over with the elders. We will have a decision late tomorrow. And whatever we decide will be final."

"Whatever," I said walking away. Spirit and them tried to follow me but I stopped them. "Ya'll go back, I want to be left alone."

"Are you sure?" Spirit asked.

"Did I stutter?"

When they walked away I was almost to my cubby when I felt someone following me. When I turned around I was staring into Wicked's eyes. I bet if his man Pop Kill didn't get arrested for fucking some chick in a car up top, he would've been with him trying to annoy me.

"If you knew what I had in my hand right now, you wouldn't be walking up on me," I told him.

He stepped back, looked at the knife and smirked. "Don't worry, I'm here for one reason and one reason only."

"And what's that?"

"To let you know that I provoked your father. I knew he would do exactly what he did and now you're finally out. Good luck staying out of jail up top. Because I have a feeling that your days are numbered."

I don't know what made me go to Concord Manor but I was there. My heart sped up in my chest when I got off of the bus and walked on the block leading to the house. I guess I was nervous because I realized that I use to live here and it brought up bad memories.

When I made it to the house I walked around back. I saw a black Rolls Royce sitting out front and I wondered who it belonged to. The grounds look kept and the outside looked better than it did when my mother was alive. I guess Jayden is doing better than I thought.

I walked in the backyard when I heard a child's voice. I realized immediately when I got closer that I was looking at my son. He didn't see me but he looked happy. His smile held me captive and made me feel as if everything was right with the world. He's my son. My only son. The only person in the world I gave life to yet I don't know him.

He was so handsome. His hair was long, wild and curly just like mine. I wiped the tear away that fell down my cheek and exhaled. I wanted to hold him so badly my stomach ached.

Cassius pushed the toy lawnmower in the yard as if nothing was wrong in the world. As if everything was right, despite his mother, *me*, not being in his life. I wanted to tell him that I was sorry for not being around but since he's only two-years-old would he be able to understand?

I was just about to make a move and go talk to him when the backdoor opened. My sister, my twin, walked out holding a large red ball. Jayden looked more beautiful than the last time I saw her and my heart leapt. I could tell without even speaking to her that she was doing well. It was because of her long black hair that flowed and the diamonds that hung from her neck and ears. I wondered what she was doing to make her money because it was obvious that she had a lot of it.

The next thing I heard broke my heart. It shattered it in a way that can't be explained unless you had a child who didn't know you. "Mommy," he said looking at her with wide eyes. "Ball!"

I felt my skin heat up and my scalp tightened. Cassius called her mommy. Not auntie or Jayden but mommy. I don't know what made me angrier. The fact that he could look at her and call her the title that was rightfully mine. Or, the fact that she allowed him too.

I hate that bitch. More than anybody I ever hated and that includes my mother. How could she do this to me? My own flesh and blood? My twin sister! I swear if I had a gun I would've shot her dead. Better yet if I had a knife I would've stabbed her with my bare hands so that she could feel my hate.

I should've never come here. I should've never allowed myself to feel this kind of pain. I know I'm not a good mother now because a good mother could never hate so much. Maybe part of me wanted him to be sad without me.

I turned around to leave.

●━━━━━━━━━━━━━━━━━━━━━━━━━━━━●

I stood before Old Man Young, The parable and the elders as I waited for the judgment. I couldn't believe I was going through all of this. They should be begging somebody to live in this funky mothafucka, instead of throwing them out. Yet here I was, homeless, and begging them to give me a few more weeks in this hellhole.

"Mad, we have given a lot of consideration to this matter," Old Man Young said. "And we realize that you have done a lot for many people here in The Catacombs. But, violence of any kind is not acceptable. You were irresponsible when you allowed your father to hurt another resident here, and for that we must hold you accountable."

I swallowed the knot in my throat. I knew what was about to go down before they even said it.

"With that said, we are exiling you from The Catacombs," Old Man Young continued. "If you refuse to go we will make life for you here difficult."

Exiling? What did that mean? Why couldn't they just tell me what the deal was using regular words? What was wrong with English?

Spirit must've sensed my confusion because he whispered in my ear, "It means you'll have to leave The Catacombs, Mad." I turned around to look at him, still a little confused. He touched my shoulder. "Them old mothafuckas putting you out."

I turned back around and faced Old Man Young and the others. They didn't know who they were fucking with. I saw where being nice got me. Nowhere. I hate this mothafucka! I hate everybody.

"So it's cool for Wicked to try to fuck my little man and lock him up in a gage. But the moment my father knocks him out it's a problem? Are you serious?"

"It's not about Wicked," Old Man Young said. "It's about the fact that you allowed an outsider into our home and in turn he hurt another member. We would've exacted the same punishment on Wicked had it been the other way around. But it wasn't. At the end of the day someone you know came into our place and hurt another."

"You just doing this because you want me to leave," I yelled at Old Man Young. "You been saying for the longest that you want me gone and now you got your wish. This shit was a set up. Even Wicked said he provoked my pops.

"It doesn't matter," Old Man Young responded. "It is time for you to leave."

I bit my inner lip. I bit down so hard I could taste my own blood. I decided not to kiss their asses anymore. If they wanted me gone then fuck it, I was going to leave. But it wouldn't be without a fight.

"When I gotta go?"

"You have one week."

I rubbed my hands together and looked at Wicked. "That's all the time I need."

CHAPTER 28

DAZE

A few days later, after Old Man Young and the elders had given Mad the verdict, Wicked, Pop Kill, Daze and Killer went into Wicked's cubby. Pop Kill was home after his short jail stint and eager to get into trouble. After the verdict they still acted as if they hit the lottery because after all of their planning, they finally got what they wanted, Mad evicted from The Catacombs.

"Do you remember seeing that bitch's face?" Wicked asked walking into his room. "I can't believe this shit."

"Yeah, she looked pretty fucked up," Daze said. "You better watch out though, man, I don't trust her."

"Why are you always worried about what somebody might do?" Wicked asked rubbing his baldhead. "She is out of here and that's all I care about."

"Yeah, baby," Killer said kissing Daze's lips. "What she gonna do to us now?"

"Besides," Wicked said patting him on the back. "I got something for you all as a token of my appreciation."

"Appreciation for what?" Pop Kill said. "I didn't even get a chance to have some fun. One minute I'm here and the next minute she's about to be out of here."

"This is for having my back," Wicked responded.

He handed them each a small baggie of heroin. "I got this out of Spirit's room. I followed him up top and caught him copping from his regular dealer. That Bitch Mad was with them."

Daze, Pop Kill and Killer's eyes widened. Immediately they started to salivate as they sat on Wicked's bed and opened the packets. In no time they cooked the dope, and loaded their needles. Wicked was supposed to save his pack to share with a female he was meeting later but he couldn't hold on any longer after seeing them cook.

"So what do you think will happen to Mad now that she gotta go?" Pop Kill asked Wicked as he tapped his vein.

"What do you think?" he responded cooking his hit. "If shit goes the way I know it will she'll be thrown out on the streets and before long thrown in jail."

Pop Kill grinned. "I would have rather have killed the slut with my bare hands instead of kicking her out. But to each his own."

"Well maybe we can hunt her down outside of The Catacombs and then you'll get your chance."

"Now you're talking," Pop Killed responded slyly.

Daze and Killer were too busy stuffing their veins to even listen to what Pop Kill or Wicked was talking about. Wicked tied Pop Kill off and Pop Kill pressed the dope into the vein. Wicked tapped his vein to inject himself. He was about to insert the needle until Pop Kill's eyes flew open.

"What's wrong, nigga?" Wicked asked.

"I think we got a bad—"

Pop Kill's sentence was cut off when he felt a lightning bolt type pain shoot through his arm. When his body started experiencing sharp pains he knew what was happening. He had received a hot shot.

The moment he fell down, Killer cried out as well as Daze.

"What's going on?" Wicked yelled looking at his friend's lying on the floor convulsing. "What the fuck is going on?"

They couldn't answer him but Mad, who was on the outside of his cubby knew exactly what happened. She got revenge on three of her enemies and there was only one more to go.

CHAPTER 29
WICKED

Wicked was sitting on his bed, rolling up a blunt laced with crack cocaine. Since Pop Kill, Daze and Killer were gone, he was alone. He still couldn't believe that they were dead. Daze and Killer had been by his side since he first made it to The Catacombs. Pop Kill came into the picture later but he still had a close bond with him. And to learn that they all died from a heroin overdose fucked him up.

He thought about how the dope was left out in the open in Spirit's room. They knew he would steal it. He couldn't bring it up because he wasn't supposed to be in Spirit's room.

He couldn't sleep ever since he and a few other West Wingers buried them in the graveyard by The Pit.

He was just about to smoke when the lights to The Catacombs went out.

He popped up from the bed. "What the fuck is going on?" he yelled out into the dark tunnel. "Why the lights go out?"

Nobody said a word and he was petrified. Hoping they'd take care of what needed to be done to get the lights back on, he decided to sit back down and finish his weed. That was until he sensed somebody behind him. Before he could move a cold knife was placed against his throat.

"I warned you didn't I?" Mad said before slicing into the flesh on his cheekbone. "But you didn't listen. Why didn't you listen?"

With the lights out Wicked felt helpless. Was she alone? Would she kill him?

"Please don't do this," Wicked begged. He wasn't acting like the arrogant bastard he usually was. "I mean...I didn't want to get you put out but you was trying to tear my family apart. Don't you realize how much I love them? They the only things I have in this world and they abandoned me all for you."

"Your family?" she laughed, before cutting into the first layer of the skin on his neck. "You don't give a fuck about anybody but yourself. What the fuck you know about family?"

"That's not true," he yelled. "I even liked you before that shit happened with Rose. You gotta believe me."

"You ain't nothing but a rat. You fucked up Gage's head so bad she still cries at night. You turned on WB and Spirit because they fucked with me and you may have been the real reason Fierce killed himself. You foul."

"Mad, listen to me," he said afraid she would cut his neck deeper, "because I can tell by your voice that you're frustrated."

"I passed frustrated a long time ago."

"Okay, just hear me out," he paused. "You gotta understand that if it wasn't for what happened to that girl getting murdered we would've been cool. I never not liked you, I just didn't know you. And so much has happened in my group that I wanted to be sure you could be trusted." Although he was being nice, he was secretly waiting for the

lights to turn back on so he could grab his knife under the bed and kill her once and for all.

"We would've never been cool, Wicked. You scum, and I don't associate with people like you."

"So what you gonna do now?" he asked with an attitude. She was unreasonable so why bother? "Kill me? Huh?"

"Naw," Mad laughed. "I'm going to stab you and let you bleed out slowly. Why do you think I went through all of the trouble to turn the lights out? So that I could cut your vocal cords and let you die of a slow death."

She was just about to finish him off when the lights came on. When she saw who was standing in Wicked's doorway she blinked twice thinking that her eyes were playing tricks on her.

They weren't.

CHAPTER 30

MAD

"Wicked, I know it's fucked up but you had it coming," Everest yelled as Wicked paced the floor of his cubby with his fists balled up. "I mean look at everything you did to her."

"This bitch just tried to kill me," he yelled as if I wasn't in the room. "Look at my neck and face! I'm the victim here remember?"

Although I was present I couldn't move. Too much was going on at the moment. What was Everest doing there? I thought she left to see the world. Why was she here trying to prevent this pussy ass nigga from telling the cops like he promised?

"Wicked, don't forget that I know about you," Everest said. "You feeling yourself right now but there isn't a person alive who knows more about you than I do. You better remember that."

A second ago this clown was pacing the floor like he was crazy and now he was stuck. His eyes were frozen and his arms hung at his sides. What did she know?

"So you would do that to me?" Wicked said. "You would turn your back on me after everything we've been through? "

"I'm just saying that what happened here just now was fucked up, but there's no need to tell the cops. You're upset but you know you can't tell the police about what goes on in our world. What do you think will happen if you told people she cut you? You'll be in jail too, Wicked because of your past. And it's not like Madjesty won't be gone in a couple of days anyway. Just let her go in peace. There's no need to kick up shit now."

Wicked looked at me. "You lucky," he said pointing my way. "Real lucky."

"Wicked, I had the knife at your throat and you still breathing. If anybody lucky it's you."

Although he was talking shit I had all intentions on finishing what I started later. Yes it was true that I was going away in a few days, but Wicked's head belonged to me and I was going to take it without any witnesses. It would just take me a little longer that's all.

Instead of waiting on a response I walked out of his cubby and toward mine. I could hear Everest's footsteps coming behind me. Why in the fuck did I allow myself to keep falling for these janky ass bitches? These dumb ass females who didn't deserve my heart?

I pushed into my cubby and she was right there. Like she still had the right to be. "Mad, can I talk to you?"

"About what, yo," I said with my back faced in her direction.

"Yo?" she said.

"What the fuck do you want?" I continued as I moved some things around in the box in my cubby.

I don't know what I was looking for but I had to do something with my hands. I couldn't look at her face. I know if I did that she would have the power over me and I didn't want her to have that control anymore. Not anymore.

"Mad, I'm sorry about leaving without saying any-thing."

I laughed. "Yeah, like always."

"What is that supposed to mean?'

I turned around and faced her. "You a runner, Everest, and I can't trust you. I'm fucked up enough as is. I don't need this mental bullshit."

"And that's why I came back. I know I'm a runner, and I don't want it to be that way anymore. You can't begin to understand how hard this is for me."

"What the fuck does that mean?"

"I know that you're leaving and I'm here to tell you that I want to go with you. With our heads together maybe we can have a future."

She stepped closer to me and put her hands on my arm. I pushed her back and she knocked against my cardboard wall. "Don't touch me. You don't got the right to touch me no more."

"Mad, what the fuck is wrong with you? You talking about me running and now that I'm here you want to leave. Can we stop playing games and work on a relationship? Please, baby. I have a feeling that we are so good for each other. Please let's just give this relationship a chance."

"Everest, we tried it and it didn't work."

"That's because we were in this dump." she looked up at the dark ceiling. "I mean look at where we live. In a tun-nel underground. A rat and bug infested tunnel. That doesn't include all of the crazy people who circle us on a daily basis. How can we expect to do anything but fight down here? That's why I want a real chance at a relationship with you. Outside of The Catacombs."

I laughed. "You want a real chance so you can what? Get a place with me and roll out when you want to see the world again? I'm not a doll, Everest. I'm not a fucking toy you play with when you bored. I got feelings."

"If you give me another chance I will never leave you again, Mad. I just need one more chance. Please. Take me with you."

I looked into her light brown eyes and they seemed to sparkle. I wanted her so bad it was ridiculous. I wanted to hold her and I also wanted her love. But Everest wasn't about shit. All she wanted to do was run game on me and fuck my mind up and that wasn't happening again.

"I'm leaving here but when I do it won't be with you."

I could see her throat bubble as if she swallowed something. "What about Pickles? You gonna leave him too?"

"I asked Spirit, Gage, WB and Fortune to look after him. I don't got any room in my world for a kid." Cassius' face flashed into my mind and I shook my head to get it out.

"So you would leave him knowing that everybody he has ever loved has abandoned him too?"

"Like I said I'm out, and I'm not letting you or anybody else get in the way of that. And, that includes Pickles."

CHAPTER 31

MAD

"Listen to me, Lil man. I'm trying to rap to you right quick," I said to Pickles as he sat on the edge of my bed. "And I want you to understand that this is really hard for me."

"Fuck you," he yelled directly into my face. "You don't like me and I don't like you!"

The little dude never kicked it to me like that before so I can't lie, I was kinda hurt. I hadn't expected him to be so mad. To tell you the truth I don't know what I expected.

"Pickles, I do like you. Why would you think like that, little man?"

"Because you leaving me by myself! You said you would never leave me."

"But Spirit is going to be here with you," I said looking into his eyes. "Along with Fortune and Gage, so don't worry. You going to be good. I promise."

"But I want you with me! You my mommy!"

Maybe it was the fact that he knew I was a woman even though I never told him before. Or maybe it was the fact that he thought of me as his mother, either way I felt worse about leaving him. I know he needs me but there's nothing I can do about it right now. I don't even know where I'm going to live when I get out of here. So how can I take care of him when my future is dark? Wanted murderers can't raise kids.

"Pickles," I said softly, "I'm not your mother, Lil man. I know I—"

"Fuck you," he yelled with tears pouring down his face. "You gonna give up on me just like my ghost mommy! I hate you! I hate everybody!"

What is a ghost mommy?

As I watched him run out of the cubby I just sat on the edge of the bed stuck. He's a kid and as bad as I feel for him, he doesn't understand the real world. He'll get over it I'm sure. He's not my responsibility. He never was.

I know all of this is true, but why do I feel like it's a bad idea?

I was about to go after him until I heard a loud scream in the tunnel. Whoever was crying sounded as if it came from the gut. Did something happen to Pickles?

I rushed through the tunnel, pushing and knocking niggas over in the process. I knew in that moment it was no way I was leaving him in this place alone. I wouldn't be able to live with myself or sleep at night due to worrying about him. I had to be there for my little man and help him out. Like Mr. Nice Guy was there for me.

But I was stopped in my tracks when Spirit blocked me, holding my little nigga's hand. It wasn't until that point that I was able to breathe. He was safe. He was okay.

I grabbed Pickles and hugged him tightly. I could smell the scent of his musty underarms but I didn't care. "You got it, lil' dude. You got it," I told him. "If I'm leaving here you coming with me too okay?"

He wrapped his little arms around my neck. "Yeah!"

I knew in that moment that I had two sons out in the world and they were going to eventually get to know each other. They were Cassius and Pickles, who's real name I didn't know yet.

When I released him I asked Spirit, "What happen? I heard somebody scream."

"That's what I was coming to tell you about."

"Well…"

"E2 found his father in a dumpster up top. He was beat to death by some kids. It's a good thing you getting out of here. Shit is getting bad for people like us."

●───●

Everest was standing over the fire at The Pit wearing this sexy yellow shirt. I wanted to talk to her, but I knew I went off on her the last time we spoke and she wouldn't be feeling me right now. I didn't treat her right when she asked to leave with me and I wanted to take every terrible thing back that I said but only if she would allow me.

Instead of being a punk, I walked over to her in front of everybody. "Everest, can I talk to you for a moment?"

She rolled her eyes and focused back on the fire. "No, I'm good." Her tone was flat and she turned her back in my direction.

I was embarrassed and looked around to see who was watching. Everyone was.

"I'll only be a second, baby." I stepped closer and whispered in her ear. "Please."

She turned around to face me. "Mad, you made your decision and I'm going to respect it. So if you don't mind I would like to be alone right now. We truly don't have anything else to talk about."

"So you trying to play me?"

"Fuck you," she said stomping away. "You don't get to hurt my feelings, make me feel worthless and then come back to me. I'm not playing your mind games anymore. If you want this thing over, then I'm going to give you exactly what you wanted. Space."

Part of me wanted to let her bounce and never talk to her again, but I did that before and it never made me feel good. I wanted to do something I normally don't do. Face how I felt and tell her straight up that I cared about her. Besides, losing Fierce made me realize how important life was.

I ran up to her and yanked her by the arm. "I'm sorry, Everest, but I can't let you go this time." She walked off and I pulled her again. "I'm sorry for how I spoke to you the other day. I know you were reaching out to me and I couldn't hear it because I was angry. I was carrying shit like a female and I hurt you in the process. But I'm done being a kid now, Everest. I'm done hurting people and I wanna make things right. Starting with my son, Pickles and you." She shook her head like she wasn't hearing me. "Can we just talk about this in private? Please."

"You just saying that."

"No I'm not, ma. I fucking love you and I made a pussy move with how I came at you that time. I know you still love me. So give me a chance to make it right." When she smiled I said. "Come holla at me in The Dump. I want to rap to you right quick."

"The Dump?" she frowned. "Since when did you start wanting to go to The Dump? You hate it there."

"Since I wanted a little privacy, and don't feel like going up top to get it."

"Are you serious, Mad?" She didn't seem as angry.

"Baby, I'm dead ass. Look, I'm gonna be gone in a few days and if you want to be with me, and my man Pickles I want you to come with me up top. I can't promise you much of a life right now, but I do know that I'm going to work my ass off trying to make things right for you. For us. The time is now for you to make the decision because I'm never coming back here."

She looked into my eyes. "Okay," she said kissing me on the lips. "I'm with you, and I don't care where we go because I know we'll be good."

"That's what's up," I said trying not to grin too hard.

Everybody cheered as we walked toward The Dump. They probably thought we were about to fuck or something. Everest giggled and threw her middle finger at everyone.

When we made it to The Dump, I picked her up and put her in the bed of the truck, which was packed with green leaves and branches. It was a little uncomfortable at first but I think we both were excited about what was about to happen.

Although I wanted to just rap to her, Everest didn't waste anytime because she pulled her shirt off and I couldn't get over how sexy her body was. She looked better than I ever imagined.

"How do I look?" She asked standing on her knees in front of me.

I swallowed. "Beautiful."

"You next," she said. "Take off your clothes."

When she moved to touch my chest I stopped her. I didn't like being touched and the fact that my breasts were cut off and replaced with a bad repair job didn't help either.

"Everest, there's something you must know about me. It didn't matter in The Catacombs because we weren't in a relationship. But I don't fuck around in that way. You gonna have to be good with not feeling me, not touching my body, or we can't make it. Maybe in time that'll change, but not right now. Okay?

She seemed slightly disappointed. "Then what do you like?"

"To please," I winked and then rubbed her braids. "Can I please you?"

"As long as you love me you can do whatever you want."

We spent the next twenty minutes fucking until the truck turned on.

And that's when my life changed.

CHAPTER 32
MAD & EVEREST

Mad and Everest laid in the back of the moving dumpster confused. To Mad's knowledge The Dump never moved so what was happening now? As they tried to conceal their bodies within the old brush, Mad's brain kicked into overdrive. She wondered how she would protect Everest if things got violent.

"Mad, I'm scared," Everest said loudly to be heard over the roar of the truck. "What's going on?"

Mad would be lying if she didn't say that she wasn't frightened too, but she couldn't let her know. She had to be strong. "I'm not sure but don't talk so loud. We don't know who these mothafuckas are or what they want. The bumps from the truck moving caused the branches inside of the bed to scratch against their arms and legs. "As soon as this bitch stops we gotta jump out okay? When I give the word be ready."

"Okay," Everest responded.

When the truck came to a complete stop Mad was preparing to instruct Everest to leap out until she heard the voices of two men.

"What the fuck was you waiting on?" Man Number One said from outside of the truck. "You could've stopped and put it back there a long time ago."

"I couldn't do it back there. Them bums were watching."

"Fuck I care about some bums?" Man Number One responded. "Half of them stay drunk anyway."

When Mad heard footsteps moving toward the back of the truck, her heart rocked. Something told her they wouldn't be happy to see her and Everest in the back since they tried to avoid them back at The Catacombs.

"Everest, put some of them brushes over your head so you can hide," Mad whispered."

Mad did the same thing and they both were concealed.

A second later a heavy item covered in clear plastic was thrown over top of their bodies. The large item was followed by twenty heavy cinder blocks, which provided crushing blows against their bodies. Just when things couldn't get any worse one of the blocks smashed Everest's arm. She placed a hand over her mouth to prevent screaming out in pain.

"Hey, did you hear something?" Man Number One said. "It sounded like it was coming from the bed of the truck."

"What the fuck are you talking about?" Man Number Two responded.

"You didn't just hear that shit?"

"Look, I put three bullets in that dead nigga's head myself. He may do a lot of things but talking ain't one of them. Now hurry up so we can dump this and make it to our meeting. You wasting time."

Man Number One threw one more block on the mound, which ripped into the flesh of Mad's head. Both she and Everest were now severely injured.

Five minutes later the truck started moving again and Mad smelled the familiar odor of rotting flesh. She'd been around enough dead bodies to be an expert on the topic. The blood from the corpse in the plastic dripped all over their bodies and dampened their face, chest and arms.

When Mad heard Everest's muffled cries she reached through the debris and rubbed the only place on her body she could touch, her wrist. She wanted to speak to Everest and tell her that she loved her but she was afraid the killers would hear them. She had to be smart and she had to be cautious if they were going to make it out of the situation alive.

They spent the next half an hour in agony with the weight of the body and cinder blocks pressing on their wounds. When the truck finally stopped Mad could smell water and fish. Suddenly the truck backed up and a beeping noise sounded off.

"That's good right there, man," Man Number One yelled. "Now dump it!"

"Mad, what's going on," Everest asked as the back of the truck raised up and the bottom lowered, moving their bodies in a sliding board type fashion.

"I don't know," Mad yelled. "But whatever happens now I want you to know that I love you."

"I love you too," Everest whimpered. "Always."

When the bed of the truck forced them along with the dead body toppling into the water, Mad knew things would get worse. Had it not been for Mr. Nice Guy showing her how to swim many years back she wouldn't have had a chance.

As Mad splashed into the water Man Number One caught a glimpse of them. "Stop it, Jeff! Stop the dump! Somebody's in the water!"

It was too late. They were gone.

CHAPTER 33
MAD AND EVEREST
PRESENT DAY

Everest's legs were not moving as much as they were moments earlier. Although she was on her back floating, while Mad doggy paddled beside her, she was growing weaker. Mad knew what was happening even if Everest didn't. God was taking yet another person she loved from her life.

When Man Number One and Man Number Two tried to shoot at them in the water they swam as quickly as possible away from them. The men couldn't catch them. But now they were in the middle of nowhere.

"What secret did you have over Wicked's head?" Mad asked. "That he was afraid you'd tell?"

"You remember that?" she smiled.

"Yes."

"He's a convicted child molester," she responded. "And I'm the only one who knew. I kept a newspaper clip in my things and he knew that if it ever got out that they wouldn't want him there."

Mad grew angrier thinking about how Pickles almost fell victim to his evil ways. And then she realized that if she never got out Pickles would be a victim again.

"Why did you pick the name Everest?" Mad asked in an attempt to think about something else. "Out of all of the names."

She giggled and in a weak voice said, "You mean after everything we've been through tonight that's the question you want to ask me?"

"I know it's weird, but I never asked you before."

"Well, I always wanted to go to Mt. Everest. The funny thing is, although I lied about everything else in my life, I didn't want to pretend I went to Mt. Everest. I wanted to actually go there you know?"

"Why?"

She exhaled. "My mother and father died on Mt. Everest when I was a kid and I believed that if I went there I could be closer to their spirits."

"Are you serious?"

She laughed. "I made a promise to you that I will never lie to you again, so yes I'm very serious. Both my mother and father were adventurers. I guess that's where I got the desire. Well one day after mountain climbing they decided to go for a bigger dream. But like they did most of the time they chose adventures, they forgot about me. I was their daughter but I was always living with their friends and family while they went on their excursions. When they died on the mountain, the woman they left me with made me her personal slave. She forced me to do stuff like cook and clean for her, and I wasn't allowed to go to school. I couldn't take it anymore so after awhile I took to the streets." She focused on the glow of the moon. "The name Everest stuck after that."

"I got it," Mad said honored that she would share her story.

Although Mad was doing a good job of hiding her own physical pain, she struggled terribly to stay conscious.

"You know I can't move my legs for much longer right?" Everest asked her. "I want to let you know that it's over for me. And without me to worry about you can swim further away and save yourself."

"So you giving up on me?"

"I could never give up on you, Mad but my body can't do it anymore."

Mad fought the anger she felt growing inside her chest. "Like I said, you giving up."

"Please don't be angry. Not now. If I'm going to die I need your love. I can't go in peace thinking that you hate me."

Mad thought about throwing so much hate on her it would feel like she was in a thunderstorm if it meant she would stay alive. But, she herself couldn't move much longer either. On more than one occasion she fought to stay out of the light that was coming to take her out of the world.

"Okay, Everest. Do what you gotta do."

"Thank you," she exhaled, kicking her legs slower. "So I'm going to stop fighting now. But before I do I want you to know something."

"What is it?" Mad wiped the blood and tears out of her eyes.

"That you are a good person and you deserve happiness."

"You don't know what the fuck you saying. I'm a menace."

"I don't know what you've done in the past but you're a great person." She paused. "And if you make it out of this you should go to your mother's grave. And when you do tell

her how you feel. Let everything off your chest, Mad. And accept your full name of Madjesty again because Mad is filled with so much rage."

Instead of telling her that she had no intentions on going anywhere near her mother's bones if she survived she said, "Okay."

"Promise me."

"If you with me I'll go."

"I'll always be with you, always. Even in death." And with that she stopped kicking her legs. Instead of letting her go under, Mad gripped her into a kiss.

"You were so good for me," Mad said looking into her eyes. "We could've been great together."

"And you were good for me too. Goodbye."

At that moment Mad saw the bright light again. It was moving closer and it was so warm and welcoming. She decided that if Everest was going to let go of life that she was going to let go too.

Madjesty shot up when she heard soft beeping sounds surrounding her. She wondered was she in hell. When she looked around the room she knew immediately that she was in the hospital and she wondered how she got there. Instead of remaining calm, she began to yell and scream at the top of her lungs. Why couldn't God just leave her alone? Why did he have to constantly butt in her life?

"Can somebody tell me what's going on?" she yelled toward the door. "Please!"

Finally a black doctor walked into the room with calming green eyes and a huge smile. "Ms. Phillips?" He held onto the clipboard in his hand with authority.

"What's going on?"

"I'm Dr. Jamal Carter and you were found in the bay and rescued. You are very lucky, young lady."

"But I wanted to die," she frowned. "Why didn't ya'll let me die?"

A look of disappointment covered the doctor's face. "Ms. Phillips, you were given the gift of life. You shouldn't feel disappointed. You should feel blessed. The wound on your head was so severe that you almost lost consciousness and drowned."

In a whisper Madjesty said, "But life ain't worth living without her. So I don't care anymore."

"Without who?"

"My girl." In life she never got to keep the girl. She was certain that this time wouldn't be any different.

"Are you speaking of Raven Hope?"

"I'm not talking about no Raven Hope," Madjesty yelled. "I'm talking about Everest."

"That's odd," he said looking through the chart. "Because Raven Hope was found in the water with you, with her arm broken."

Madjesty stopped breathing momentarily. She didn't know Everest's real name before that moment because Everest never volunteered the information. Could Everest be Raven Hope?

Mad leaned closer. "Is this Raven chick still alive?"

"Sure she is," he smiled. "She is equally as lucky and she kept asking about you."

Mad was done. All of her life she had people taken from her and now things were different. "How was she found?"

"Me and my people found her," a short Latino man said as he walked into the room. "In my boat while we were searching for you."

"And who are you?" the doctor asked suspiciously. The man before him had three other white men with him and he didn't look trustworthy. There was a dark air surrounding him and the doctor was uncomfortable.

"My name is Rick and I'm Jace's father. Madjesty and I have business."

Mad and Everest sat on Rick's sofa in his home. Although she'd never been there before, she could tell that he had an ongoing relationship with her twin sister Jayden. Pictures of Rick and Jayden together were all over the living room and there was even a picture of her son Cassius on the mantle. Cassius looked healthy but more than anything he looked happy and her heart ached slightly. No matter what it would take, she knew she had to get her son back.

"I don't know why Jace would do that." Mad said to Rick due to a conversation they were having. Mad's arm was around Everest as she struggled to get comfortable on his couch.

"I don't know either, but he did leave you money in his life insurance policy," he responded sitting in the recliner across from them. He was holding a cup of tea and his baby finger was hyper extended. "I'm told he opened the policy when he found out that Jayden was his daughter."

"But I'm not his biological child so why would he include me?"

"I know," he replied. Mad couldn't be sure, but she detected a small sense of annoyance from him. "I'm quite aware of the situation. I know that Kali is your father, and Jace is Jayden's, but that didn't stop him from leaving you a half of million dollars."

Although Everest was happy about the policy, because the money meant that they could start a new life, Mad was rightfully skeptical. The man's mannerisms showed that he didn't want her to have the cash, even though it was left in her name. In Mad's opinion he didn't seem to respect Jace's decision.

"Well what if I don't want it?" Mad asked.

"What?" Everest yelled rotating her head in Mad's direction. "Why wouldn't you want the money? He gave it to you."

"I'm talking to the man, baby," Mad said respectfully but firmly. She focused back on him. "What if I don't want the paper?"

"Then you can sign it over to me," he smiled for the first time that evening. He placed the tea on the glass table in front of him. "But we can't do anything with the cash until you release it to us."

"If I wanted it, when would the money be available?" Mad asked.

"In six months after we let the insurance company know."

"Jayden get her half yet?"

"We're working with her to get her money," he said with a slight attitude. He was trying to work with Mad in the calmest way possible but it wasn't working. He was definite-

ly annoyed. "Since I'm in charge of his estate I have to care for all of these matters."

"Is that why you kept sending people to The Catacombs dressed in suits and shit, looking for me? So that I could give you the money?"

"You could look at it like that."

"Did you come to the Gates Motel too?"

"Yes, but it's important that you know that this isn't all about the money," he chuckled. "It's about the fact that Jace wasn't thinking straight when he put you on this policy. He felt obligated for whatever reason and we knew that if we spoke to you that we could convince you to see things our way."

"Convince huh?" Mad responded.

"Yes and you should know that I can be very persuasive."

Silence.

"What about Wicked? You said that he told your people that I was in The Dump, and that's how your people followed the truck to the bay. But where is he now?"

"We have him pinned up at the moment. With your word we will release him. It's just that from what he told my men, who he believed were officers, he was going to cause problems for you."

"And you needed me out of jail to sign these papers?"

"Yes. But I must admit, we were also concerned that he was going to snitch on you. And even though there is the matter of money, we have no respect for men like that."

"What a snake," Everest said.

"Your lady is correct," Rick responded. "What do you want done with him?"

Mad thought about it long and hard. When she real-ized all he had done to her she wanted revenge. "Kill him."

"We can take care of that problem for you. And in turn you can help us handle this matter with the money. You are going to sign it back over to his family right? Where it right-fully belongs?"

Mad looked at his slicked back hair and his lowered eyes. She didn't trust him. She didn't trust him one bit and she certainly didn't want him around her son.

"I'll make a decision on what I'm going to do with my money later," Mad responded. "But first I want Wicked murdered."

CHAPTER 34

MAD

Me, Everest and Pickles were standing outside of a police station. The sun shined brightly. Although I knew what I had to do, for a chance at a better life, neither me or Everest was happy about it.

"Mad, why are you doing this?" Everest asked as she placed her hands on the sides of my face. "Let's just run away from it all!"

"I can't, baby," I said stroking her arms. "If I thought that was the answer I would have no problem doing it. But I'm tired of living like this. I want something better."

"But why not just run?"

"Because if we are going to have that money and a chance at a real life, I have to turn myself in and deal with this shit. And since I made you power of attorney, when the money comes in six months just get me a good lawyer if they don't let me out of jail. That's what we got to do but running away is not the option anymore."

"I hate you so fucking much right now," she yelled dropping her hands by her sides. "You know Pickles is going to be sad when you leave. He'll probably be up all hours of the night crying and shit. Just stay with me, Mad. Stay with us."

"I'm not gonna be crying," Pickles interjected. "Smooth Pop told me I gotta be strong. So I'ma be strong since I'm in charge now."

I told him to call me Smooth Pop instead of mommy because mommy made me uncomfortable.

I ruffled his curly hair. "That's my little man. Being all responsible and shit."

"I'm glad he's strong," she said under her breath. "Because I'm an emotional wreck. I don't know why but something tells me this situation ain't going to end good."

"Listen, baby, I'm innocent," Mad said seriously. "I did not kill that chick. And if justice is on my side, I should be able to convince a jury of my peers that I'm telling the truth."

She looked away. "Mad, when are you going to realize that the laws of this land don't work for black people? If you go into that jail you never coming out."

"Well for the chance to keep you, Pickles and get my son, I'm going to take a shot."

"Whatever, Mad." She folded her hands over her chest.

I raised her chin and looked into her eyes. "Just be good for me. And don't worry, my folks is real cool. Sugar and Krazy are family and they got you. They know what you and Pickles mean to me."

"That's what you say but if you ask me the Sugar girl acts like she wants to fuck you or something. I could see it in her eyes the moment they ran into us when we were eating at IHOP."

Sometimes women notice too much and that scares me. Although Sugar did want to fuck with me back in the day, we didn't push off because she was my friend and I wasn't about that. And by the time I considered dealing with her on the low, I discovered that she was with Krazy.

I was just grateful that when I ran into Krazy and Sugar, they agreed to let us live with them. Because we couldn't go back to The Catacombs and even if we could I didn't feel comfortable. I never found out who the men were in the dump truck and it messed me up. Without Krazy and Sugar giving us a room in their two-bedroom apartment until I got on my feet, I didn't have anywhere safe for Everest and Pickles to go until I got my cash. Krazy and Sugar's place was it.

"Sugar cool. You just make sure you don't let Krazy or any of my other friends try to push up on you. They sick like that," I joked.

"Ain't nobody touching this pussy but you," she said wiping the tears from her eyes. "You just hurry back to me, Mad. I'm not the kind of girl who can stay in wait for too long."

⎯⎯⎯⎯⎯⎯⎯⎯⎯⎯⎯⎯⎯⎯⎯⎯⎯⎯⎯⎯⎯⎯⎯⎯⎯⎯⎯

When I walked into the police station I started to run back out. I realized the moment I saw the shine of their gold police badges that I didn't want to be here. I didn't want to leave Everest and Pickles and I wanted to get Cassius back. But I couldn't run the risk of the cops chasing me around anymore. For once I wanted a chance at a real life and I had to fight and be responsible. For some reason I think everything I went through in The Catacombs got me ready to take care of myself and my family.

I slowly walked up to the white police officer at the counter who was holding a pen and said, "Hello," I cleared my throat. "My name is Madjesty Phillips."

"So," he shrugged looking at the papers in front of him.

I figured my name would be enough but I guess I was wrong. "I'm here about the Rose Midland girl who was murdered awhile back."

He looked up at me with suspicious eyes. Now I had his attention. "What about her?" He threw the pen on the counter.

"I'm turning myself in," I said. "And you need to hurry up and take me before I run out of here and change my mind."

He frowned. "Get the fuck out of my face, kid I don't have time for this shit," he picked the pen up. "With the case load I have in front of me right now, that's the last thing I need." He went back to reading his papers.

What the fuck was wrong with this pig? I was here to turn myself in and he acted like I was a bum asking for five bucks. "So you not gonna arrest me?"

"For what? Craig Urey was arrested six months ago for the crime." He shook his head. "He was found wearing nothing but a blue jean jacket with a sun on the back." He shook his head again. "Sick ass pervert. His DNA was found inside of her body and under her fingernails. It was an easy case. Where have you been? Living in a hole or something?"

My jaw dropped.

When I left the police station I looked more into the case of Rose Midland. I couldn't believe that the dude who lived in The Catacombs years earlier had raped and killed her and tried to frame me by putting her blood on my shirt and hands. The worst part was I had been living in a tunnel because I was afraid to get arrested when it was for nothing. I could've left a long time ago. I wasted a bunch of my life on this shit. But if I didn't stay there, I would not have met Everest or Pickles.

And now Everest was driving Pickles and me to some place I really didn't want to go. But promises were promises and she remembered all of them.

"You go ahead, baby," Everest said to me as we sat in our new car. It was a bucket that we picked up from an auction until all of my money came. "I think you need to do this alone."

"I don't even know what to say to her," I said looking at the graveyard.

"Just talk from your heart," she said. "She can't hurt you anymore. Nobody can. Maybe it's time to let your pain go."

I looked back at Pickles who was smiling. I must admit, the little youngin' cleaned up good. He was rocking some fresh J's that I bought him and a black North Face coat.

"We'll be here when you get back," he told me.

As I eased out of the car I walked slowly toward my mother's grave. I didn't want to come here but Everest kept talking about the promise I made to her when I thought we were about to die in the water. I wondered if I would've agreed to the same thing had I realized that she would take me so seriously.

When I found her gray headstone that read Harmony Phillips I looked down at it. "Hey, ma."

Silence.

"Wow, I never thought I'd call you ma again but I guess I was wrong."

I looked down at the grass and several bushels of dried roses rested near her headstone. I guess Jayden had been here.

"I'm here to tell you how you made me feel. It's not like I give a fuck anymore though, cause I'm doing this mainly for my girl." I looked back at the car and Everest and Pickles were staring at me. I cleared my throat and focused back on the grave. "You were a monster. A fucking monster and I hated you so much. I hated you for all of the days you pressed irons against Jayden and my skin. I hated you for all the days and nights we went hungry and watched you cook for dudes you fucked. I hated you for all of the men you had sex with in the living room because you were too trifling and drunk to go in your own room. I hated you for making my sister and me steal from the grocery store for food, only for you to sell it for bottles of liquor. I hated you so much."

Tears started pouring down my face and I grew angrier.

"All I wanted you to do was love me. I just wanted you for one time, for one day, to tell me you cared. Would it have been so much to ask? Would it have been so much for you not to come home drunk? But you didn't care. You didn't give a fuck! You were selfish but you know what? I...I....I forgive you."

The tears rolled out of my eyes harder and for some reason I felt powerful.

"I forgive you for not loving me, because maybe you didn't know how. Maybe nobody showed you how to be a mother. Maybe nobody showed you how to love us or yourself." I wiped the tears from my eyes and exhaled.

"Anyway," I sighed. "I'm a mother now. Well, I'm actually a Smooth Pop." I laughed. "And I'm going to be in my boys' lives and they gonna always know that I love them. I'm going to inspire them, fight for them, and let them know how I feel about them everyday. And maybe, just maybe, you'll be proud of me too. Bye, mom. You don't have to come into my dreams anymore. I'm giving you permission to rest in peace. "

●━━━━━━━━━━━━━━━━━●

I was at The Pit with the members of The Catacombs. Everest was right, after I let the hate go I had for my mother in my heart I felt stronger. It was as if nobody else could hurt me. I didn't tell Everest but I was glad I agreed to go to the grave. All I wanted to do now was get the money that Jace left me, get us some place to live and get Cassius.

I was invited to The Catacombs for a barbeque at The Pit. They were having for Everest and me. They were happy that we were alive since they heard about what happened to us in The Dump. At the moment the place where the truck use to be was empty, leaving The Catacombs exposed in two ways now.

It turned out that since The Dump was moved, the dead bodies we kept spotting stopped showing up in The Catacombs. I guess whoever they were, they were using our home as their graveyard for years and we didn't know it.

Although I appreciated the offer for the celebration, I didn't feel comfortable there anymore. But Everest was so serious about going back and saying goodbye and I wanted to make her happy that I agreed. All I wanted to do was say my farewells and leave. After an hour passed, me, Everest and Pickles were about to go back to Krazy and Sugar's house. That is until I saw a familiar face.

At first I didn't know it was him, because he looked much cleaner than he did the last time I saw him. But the closer he got I knew exactly who he was. It was Wicked and he had a gun in his hand.

He didn't spend anytime talking or saying what he was about to do. He just aimed in my direction and I froze. Because right next to me was two of the people I loved most, Everest and Pickles and I was afraid for their lives.

He fired multiple times at me, and I can tell you this, some of them bullets hit.

EPILOGUE
Five Months Later

Madjesty stood in the doorway of the bedroom she shared with Everest and Pickles in Krazy's house. Although life was different for them, it didn't change Mad's love for her.

When the bullets flew out of Wicked's gun, one tore into Spirit's shoulder, one hit the trashcan and ricocheted inside of it. The last caught Everest in the left eye. But fragments from the bullet caught her right eye too and' completely removed her eyesight.

Everest took her new condition hard, and her attitude toward life totally changed. She cried most nights and was angry the others. No matter how many stories Pickles would read to her at night, or how many kisses Mad would plant on her face, it could never return her eyesight and for that Everest was bitter.

"How she doing?" Krazy asked walking up behind Mad as she observed Everest and Pickles sleeping in the bed.

"Not good," Mad whispered. "One part of me is happy she survived but the other part of me wonders if death would not have been better for her." She continued to look at her. "She's miserable, man, and I don't know what to do."

"Don't talk about death being better, Mad," Krazy responded. "Death is never better."

"That's what you say."

"It's the truth. Anyway, some mail came for you today." He handed Mad the envelope.

She observed it briefly. Although she was learning to read, she was a long way away from being fluent. "Who is it from?"

"It's from the Prince George's county circuit court."

Mad didn't open it right away because she figured it was the petition she filed to get Cassius back. She didn't want to rip the bond Cassius had with Jayden either. Although they had their problems, she knew he loved Jayden. So Mad met with Jayden and they agreed that Cassius should be returned to Madjesty at once. Besides, Mad was coming into a lot of money and would have the means to care for her child. Jayden's only wish was that she could continue to see her nephew and Mad respected it.

Besides, Mad and Cassius were destined to be reunited. The moment Cassius saw Mad's face, he couldn't keep his little hands off of her. To make things sweeter, Cassius and Pickles got along just like Mad knew that they would. It was as if they were long lost brothers. The only problem Mad had in her life at the moment was that her girlfriend was blind and depressed.

"I'll open it in a second," Mad said stuffing the envelope in her back pocket and then leaning on the doorframe. *"I wanted to say something to you, Krazy,"* she looked over at him, *"I appreciate you letting us stay here."*

"Nigga, please," he said brushing it off. *"Do you realize how much I love having you here? We were worried about you before we ran into you that day, man. Real talk."* He exhaled. *"Besides, ever since you and your fam moved in, me and Sugar don't fight as much. I don't know what's*

up with Sugar but it's like she wants something she can't have. The only thing is, she's not telling me what."

When Krazy made that statement he looked dead into Mad's eyes. It was evident what he was saying. That after all this time Sugar was still sweet on Mad and he wanted to be sure that Mad respected their relationship.

So she answered it in the best way possible without bringing extreme light to the situation. "I'm sure shit will be cool between you and Sugar. I didn't think I would find somebody to love again but now that I have I'm not letting anything come in between our bond. My focus is Everest and my boys."

"I hope so," he said looking at Everest and Pickles sleeping too. "But look, I wanted to rap to you about something."

"What's up?"

"I been thinking about what you said about how your girl got shot and what not, and something don't feel right to me."

"What you mean?" she frowned. "After he shot her I dealt with him. Wicked is dead now. I didn't want to tell you because I didn't want you involved. I almost sliced his head clear off of his shoulders and The Catacombs members and me fixed it so that his body will never be found. What's better than that?"

"I can dig it but that's not my issue." Krazy paused. "I remember when you were saying that Jace's father had him in his custody."

"He did, but when I asked him why he hadn't killed him, he said he got away."

"And you believe that?" Krazy continued.

"What you trying to say?"

"I'm saying that Rick wanted you to sign over that life insurance money and you said you wasn't. And that you needed the paper to start a new life. So how do you know Rick didn't get mad and send Wicked to execute you? I mean think about it for a second, with you out of the picture, Rick would be clear to control the money. And Jayden is so far up Rick's ass that I wouldn't be surprised if she gave him her half too."

What Krazy said was so clear that Mad immediately grew angry. She would've put one and two together herself, if she didn't have to care for Everest and Pickles.

"I hear what you saying, but even if I died the money still wouldn't go to him. It would go to Cassius since he's my son."

Krazy slapped her on the back. "Well it's a good thing you about to get custody of your son then, because he needs to be safe and away from Jayden who Rick controls."

"Hey, man, before you bounce read this for me." She handed him the envelope.

Krazy ripped it open and read it. He shook his head and looked at her in disappointment.

"What is it, man?" Mad asked.

"We spoke too soon. Your sister is taking you to court for the sole custody of Cassius Phillips. I guess it's time to get ready for the fight of your life."

COMING SOON

13 FLAVORS

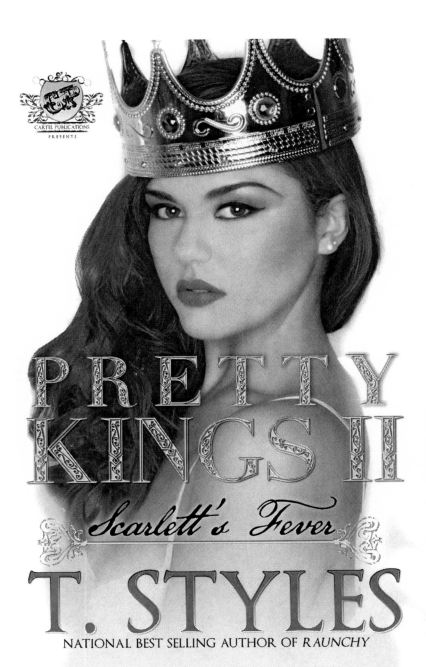

CARTEL PUBLICATIONS
PRESENTS

PRETTY KINGS II

Scarlett's Fever

T. STYLES

NATIONAL BEST SELLING AUTHOR OF *RAUNCHY*

SILENCE

OF THE

NINE

T. STYLES

NATIONAL BEST SELLING AUTHOR OF *RAUNCHY*

The Cartel Collection
Established in January 2008
We're growing stronger by the month!!!
www.thecartelpublications.com

Cartel Publications Order Form
Inmates ONLY get novels for $10.00 per book!

Titles	*Fee*
Shyt List	$15.00
Shyt List 2	$15.00
Pitbulls In A Skirt	$15.00
Pitbulls In A Skirt 2	$15.00
Pitbulls In A Skirt 3	$15.00
Pitbulls In A Skirt 4	$15.00
Victoria's Secret	$15.00
Poison	$15.00
Poison 2	$15.00
Hell Razor Honeys	$15.00
Hell Razor Honeys 2	$15.00
A Hustler's Son 2	$15.00
Black And Ugly As Ever	$15.00
Year of The Crack Mom	$15.00
The Face That Launched a Thousand Bullets	$15.00
The Unusual Suspects	$15.00
Miss Wayne & The Queens of DC	$15.00
Year of The Crack Mom	$15.00
Paid in Blood	$15.00
Shyt List III	$15.00
Shyt List **IV**	$15.00
Raunchy	$15.00
Raunchy 2	$15.00
Raunchy 3	$15.00
Jealous Hearted	$15.00
Quita's Dayscare Center	$15.00
Quita's Dayscare Center 2	$15.00
Shyt List V	$15.00
Deadheads	$15.00
Pretty Kings	$15.00
Drunk & Hot Girls	$15.00
Hersband Material	$15.00
Upscale Kittens	$15.00
Wake & Bake Boys	$15.00
Young & Dumb	$15.00
Tranny 911	$15.00
First Comes Love Then Comes Murder	$15.00
Young & Dumb: Vyce's Getback	$15.00
Luxury Tax	$15.00
Mad Maxxx	$15.00

Please add $4.00 per book for shipping and handling.
The Cartel Publications * P.O. Box 486 * Owings Mills * MD * 21117

Name: _____

Address: _____

City/State: _____

Contact # & Email: _____

Please allow 5-7 business days for delivery. The Cartel is not responsible for prison orders rejected.

Personal Checks Are Not Accepted.

CPSIA information can be obtained at www.ICGtesting.com
Printed in the USA
LVOW08s0931100515

437935LV00001B/261/P